Adela Cathcart

George MacDonald

Contents

ADELA CATHCART

BY

George MacDonald

CHAPTER I.
MY UNCLE PETER.--CONTINUED.

It was resolved that on the same evening, Chrissy should tell my uncle her story. We went out for a walk together; and though she was not afraid to go, the least thing startled her. A voice behind her would make her turn pale and look hurriedly round. Then she would smile again, even before the colour had had time to come back to her cheeks, and say--'What a goose I am! But it is no wonder.' I could see too that she looked down at her nice clothes now and then with satisfaction. She does not like me to say so, but she does not deny it either, for Chrissy can't tell a story even about her own feelings. My uncle had given us five pounds each to spend, and that was jolly. We bought each other such a lot of things, besides some for other people. And then we came home and had dinner ***tete-a-tete*** in my uncle's dining-room; after which we went up to my uncle's room, and sat over the fire in the twilight till his afternoon-nap was over, and he was ready for his tea. This was ready for him by the time he awoke. Chrissy got up on the bed beside him; I got up at the foot of the bed, facing her, and we had the tea-tray and plenty of ***etceteras*** between us.

"'Oh! I ***am*** happy!' said Chrissy, and began to cry.

"'So am I, my darling!' rejoined Uncle Peter, and followed her example.

"'So am I,' said I, 'but I don't mean to cry about it.' And then I did.

"We all had one cup of tea, and some bread and butter in silence after this. But when Chrissy had poured out the second cup for Uncle Peter, she began of her own accord to tell us her story.

"'It was very foggy when we came out of school that afternoon, as you may remember, dear uncle.'

"'Indeed I do,' answered Uncle Peter with a sigh.

"'I was coming along the way home with Bessie--you know Bessie, uncle--and we stopped to look in at a bookseller's window where the gas was lighted. It was full of Christmas things already. One of them I thought very pretty, and I was standing staring at it, when all at once I saw that a big drabby woman had poked herself in between Bessie and me. She was staring in at the window too. She was so nasty that I moved away a little from her, but I wanted to have one more look at the picture. The woman came close to me. I moved again. Again she pushed up to me. I looked in her face, for I was rather cross by this time. A horrid feeling, I cannot tell you what it was like, came over me as soon as I saw her. I know how it was now, but I did not know then why I was frightened. I think she saw I was frightened; for she instantly walked against me, and shoved and hustled me round the corner--it was a corner-shop--and before I knew, I was in another street. It was dark and narrow. Just at the moment a man came from the opposite side and joined the woman. Then they caught hold of my hands, and before my fright would let me speak, I was deep into the narrow lane, for they ran with me as fast as they could. Then I began to scream, but they said such horrid words that I was forced to hold my tongue; and in a minute more they had me inside a dreadful house, where the plaster was dropping away from the walls, and the skeleton-ribs of the house were looking through. I was nearly dead with terror and disgust. I don't think it was a bit less dreadful to me from having dim recollections of having known such places well enough at one time of my life. I think that only made me the more frightened, because so the place seemed to have a claim upon me. What if I ought to be there after all, and these dreadful creatures were my father and mother!

"'I thought they were going to beat me at once, when the woman, whom I suspected to be my aunt, began to take off my frock. I was dreadfully frightened, but I could not cry. However it was only my clothes that they wanted. But I cannot tell you how frightful it was. They took almost everything I had on, and it was only when I began to scream in despair-- sit still, Charlie, it's all over now--that they stopped, with a nod to each other, as much as to say--'we can get the rest afterwards.' Then they put a filthy frock on me; brought me some dry bread to eat; locked the door, and left me. It was nearly dark now. There was no fire. And all my warm clothes were gone.--Do sit still, Charlie.--I was dreadfully cold. There was a wretched-looking bed in one corner, but I think I would have died of cold rather than get into it. And the air in the place was frightful. How long I sat there in the dark, I don't know.'

"'What did you do all the time?' said I.

"'There was only one thing to be done, Charlie. I think that is a foolish question to ask.'

"'Well, what ***did*** you do, Chrissy?'

"'Said my prayers, Charlie.'

"'And then?'

"'Said them again.'

"'And nothing else?'

"'Yes; I tried to get out of the window, but that was of no use; for I could not open it. And it was one story high at least.'

"'And what did you do next?'

"'Said over all my hymns.'

"'And then--what ***did*** you do next?'

"'Why do you ask me so many times?'

"'Because I want to know.'

"'Well, I will tell you.--I left my prayers alone; and I began at the beginning, and I told God the whole story, as if He had known nothing about it, from the very beginning when Uncle Peter found me on the crossing, down to the minute when I was talking there to Him in the dark.'

"'Ah! my dear,' said my uncle, with faltering voice, 'you felt better after that, I daresay. And here was I in despair about you, and thought He did not care for any of us. I was very naughty, indeed.'

"'And what next?' I said.

"'By and by I heard a noise of quarrelling in the street, which came nearer and nearer. The door was burst open by some one falling against it. Blundering steps came up the stairs. The two who had robbed me, evidently tipsy, were trying to unlock the door. At length they succeeded, and tumbled into the room.'

"'Where is the unnatural wretch,' said the woman, 'who ran away and left her own mother in poverty and sickness?'--

"'Oh! uncle, can it be that she is my mother?' said Chrissy, interrupting herself.

"'I don't think she is,' answered Uncle Peter. 'She only wanted to vex you, my lamb. But it doesn't matter whether she is or not.'

"'Doesn't it, uncle?--I am ashamed of her.'

"'But you are God's child. And He can't be ashamed of you. For He gave you the mother you had, whoever she was, and never asked you which you would have. So you need not mind. We ought always to like best to be just what God has made us.'

"'I am sure of that, uncle.--Well, she began groping about to find me, for it was very dark. I sat quite still, except for trembling all over, till I felt her hands on me, when I jumped up, and she fell on the floor. She began swearing dreadfully, but did not try to get up. I crept away to another corner. I heard the man snoring, and the woman breathing loud. Then I felt my way to the door, but, to my horror, found the man lying across it on the floor, so that I could not open it. Then I believe I cried for the first time. I was nearly frozen to death, and there was all the long night to bear yet. How I got through it, I cannot tell. It did go away. Perhaps God destroyed some of it for me. But when the light began to come through the window, and show me all the filth of the place, the man and the woman lying on the floor, the woman with her head cut and covered with blood, I began to feel that the darkness had been my friend. I felt this yet more when I saw the state of my own dress, which I had forgotten in the dark. I felt as if I had done some shameful thing, and wanted to follow the darkness, and hide in the skirts of it. It was an old gown of some woollen stuff, but it was impossible to tell what, it was so dirty and worn. I was ashamed that even those drunken creatures should wake and see me in it. But the light would come, and it came and came, until at last it waked them up, and the first words were so dreadful! They quarrelled and swore at each other and at me, until I almost thought there couldn't be a God who would let that go on so, and never stop it. But I suppose He wants them to stop, and doesn't care to stop it Himself, for He could easily do that of course, if He liked.'

"'Just right, my darling!' said Uncle Peter with emotion.

"Chrissy saw that my uncle was too much excited by her story although he tried not to show it, and with a wisdom which I have since learned to appreciate, cut it short.

"'They did not treat me cruelly, though, the worst was, that they gave me next to nothing to eat. Perhaps they wanted to make me thin and wretched looking, and I believe they succeeded.--Charlie, you'll turn over the cream, if you don't sit still.--Three days passed this way. I have thought all over it, and I think they were a little puzzled how to get rid of me. They had no doubt watched me for a long time, and now they had got my clothes, they were afraid.--At last one night they took me out. My aunt, if aunt she is, was respectably dressed--that is, comparatively, and the man had a great-coat on, which covered his dirty clothes. They helped me into a cart which stood at the door, and drove off. I resolved to watch the way we went. But we took so many turnings through narrow streets before we came out in a main road, that I soon found it was all one mass of confusion in my head; and it was too dark to read any of the names of the streets, for the man kept as much in the middle of the road as possible. We drove some miles, I should think, before we stopped at the gate of a small house with a big porch, which stood alone. My aunt got out and went up to the house, and was admitted. After a few minutes, she returned, and making me get out, she led me up to the house, where an elderly lady stood, holding the door half open. When we reached it, my aunt gave me a sort of shove in, saying to the lady, 'There she is.' Then she said to me: 'Come now be a good girl and don't tell lies,' and turning hastily, ran down the steps, and got into the cart at the gate, which drove off at once the way we had come. The lady looked at me from head to foot sternly but kindly too, I thought, and so glad was I to find myself clear of those dreadful creatures, that I burst out crying. She instantly began to read me a lecture on the privilege of being placed with Christian people, who would instruct me how my soul might be saved, and teach me to lead an honest and virtuous life. I tried to say that I had led an honest life. But as often as I opened my mouth to tell anything about myself or my uncle, or, indeed, to say anything at all, I was stopped by her saying--'Now don't tell lies. Whatever you do, don't tell lies.' This shut me up quite. I could not speak when I knew she would not believe me. But I did not cry, I only felt my face get very hot, and somehow my back-bone grew longer, though I felt my eyes fixed on the ground.

"'But,' she went on, 'you must change you dress. I will show you the way to your room, and you will find a print gown there, which I hope you will keep clean. And above all things don't tell lies.'

"Here Chrissy burst out laughing, as if it was such fun to be accused of lying;

but presently her eyes filled, and she made haste to go on.

"'You may be sure I made haste to put on the nice clean frock, and, to my delight, found other clean things for me as well. I declare I felt like a princess for a whole day after, notwithstanding the occupation. For I soon found that I had been made over to Mrs. Sprinx, as a servant of all work. I think she must have paid these people for the chance of reclaiming one whom they had represented as at least a great liar. Whether my wages were to be paid to them, or even what they were to be, I never heard. I made up my mind at once that the best thing would be to do the work without grumbling, and do it as well as I could, for that would be doing no harm to anyone, but the contrary, while it would give me the better chance of making my escape. But though I was determined to get away the first opportunity, and was miserable when I thought how anxious you would all be about me, yet I confess it was such a relief to be clean and in respectable company, that I caught myself singing once or twice the very first day. But the old lady soon stopped that. She was about in the kitchen the greater part of the day till almost dinner-time, and taught me how to cook and save my soul both at once.'

"'Indeed,' interrupted Uncle Peter, 'I have read receipts for the salvation of the soul that sounded very much as if they came out of a cookery-book.' And the wrinkles of his laugh went up into his night-cap. Neither Chrissy nor I understood this at the time, but I have often thought of it since.

"Chrissy went on:

"'I had finished washing up my dinner-things, and sat down for a few minutes, for I was tired. I was staring into the fire, and thinking and thinking how I should get away, and what I should do when I got out of the house, and feeling as if the man and the woman were always prowling about it, and watching me through the window, when suddenly I saw a little boy in a corner of the kitchen, staring at me with great brown eyes. He was a little boy, perhaps about six years old, with a pale face, and very earnest look. I did not speak to him, but waited to see what he would do. A few minutes passed, and I forgot him. But as I was wiping my eyes, which would get wet sometimes, notwithstanding my good-fortune, he came up to me, and said in a timid whisper,

"'Are you a princess?'

"'What makes you think that?' I said.

"'You have got such white hands,' he answered.

"'No, I am not a princess,' I said.

"'Aren't you Cinderella?'

"'No, my darling,' I replied; 'but something like her; for they have stolen me away from home and brought me here. I wish I could get away.'

"'And here I confess I burst into a down right fit of crying.

"'Don't cry,' said the little fellow, stroking my cheek. 'I will let you out some time. Shall you be able to find your way home all by yourself?'

"'Yes I think so,' I answered; but at the same time, I felt very doubtful about it, because I always fancied those people watching, me. But before either of us spoke again, in came Mrs. Sprinx.

"'You naughty boy! What business have you to make the servant neglect her work?'

"'For I was still sitting by the fire, and my arm was round the dear little fellow, and his head was leaning on my shoulder.

"'She's not a servant, auntie!' cried he, indignantly. 'She's a real princess, though of course she won't own to it.'

"'What lies you have been telling the boy! You ought to be ashamed of yourself. Come along directly. Get the tea at once, Jane.'

"'My little friend went with his aunt, and I rose and got the tea. But I felt much lighter-hearted since I had the sympathy of the little boy to comfort me. Only I was afraid they would make him hate me. But, although I saw very little of him the rest of the time, I knew they had not succeeded in doing so; for as often as he could, he would come sliding up to me, saying 'How do you do, princess?'and then run away, afraid of being seen and scolded.

"'I was getting very desperate about making my escape, for there was a high wall about the place, and the gate was always locked at night. When Christmas-Eve came, I was nearly crazy with thinking that to-morrow was uncle's birthday; and that I should not be with him. But that very night, after I had gone to my room, the door opened, and in came little Eddie in his nightgown, his eyes looking very bright and black over it.

"'There, princess!' said he, 'there is the key of the gate. Run.'

"'I took him in my arms and kissed him, unable to speak. He struggled to get free, and ran to the door. There he turned and said:

"'You will come back and see me some day--will you not?'

"'That I will,' I answered.

"'That you shall,' said Uncle Peter.

"'I hid the key, and went to bed, where I lay trembling. As soon as I was sure they must be asleep, I rose and dressed. I had no bonnet or shawl but those I had come in; and though they disgusted me, I thought it better to put them on. But I dared not unlock the street-door for fear of making a noise. So I crept out of the kitchen-window, and then I got out at the gate all safe. No one was in sight. So I locked it again, and threw the key over. But what a time of fear and wandering about I had in the darkness, before I dared to ask any one the way. It was a bright, clear night; and I walked very quietly till I came upon a great wide common. The sky, and the stars, and the wideness frightened me, and made me gasp at first. I felt as if I should fall away from everything into nothing. And it was so lonely! But then I thought of God, and in a moment I knew that what I had thought loneliness was really the presence of God. And then I grew brave again, and walked on. When the morning dawned, I met a bricklayer going to his work; and found that I had been wandering away from London all the time; but I did not mind that. Now I turned my face towards it, though not the way I had come. But I soon got dreadfully tired and faint, and once I think I fainted quite. I went up to a house, and asked for a piece of bread, and they gave it to me, and I felt much better after eating it. But I had to rest so often, and got so tired, and my feet got so sore, that--you know how late it was before I got home to my darling uncle.'

"'And me too!' I expostulated.

"'And you, too, Charlie,' she answered; and we all cried over again.

"'This shan't happen any more!' said my uncle.

"After tea was over, he asked for writing things, and wrote a note, which he sent off.

"The next morning, about eleven, as I was looking out of the window, I saw a carriage drive up and stop at our door.

"'What a pretty little brougham!' I cried. 'And such a jolly horse! Look here, Chrissy!'

"Presently Uncle Peter's bell rang, and Miss Chrissy was sent for. She came down again radiant with pleasure.

"'What do you think, Charlie! That carriage is mine--all my own. And I am to go to school in it always. Do come and have a ride in it.'

"You may be sure I was delighted to do so.

"'Where shall we go?' I said.

"'Let us ask uncle if we may go and see the little darling who set me free.'

"His consent was soon obtained, and away we went. It was a long drive, but we enjoyed it beyond everything. When we reached the house, we were shown into the drawing-room.

"There was Mrs. Sprinx and little Eddie. The lady stared; but the child knew Cinderella at once, and flew into her arms.

"'I knew you were a princess!' he cried. 'There, auntie!'

"But Mrs. Sprinx had put on an injured look, and her hands shook very much.

"'Really, Miss Belper, if that is your name, you have behaved in a most unaccountable way. Why did you not tell me, instead of stealing the key of the gate, and breaking the kitchen window? A most improper way for a young lady to behave--to run out of the house at midnight!'

"'You forget, madam,' replied Chrissy, with more dignity than I had ever seen her assume, 'that as soon as ever I attempted to open my mouth, you told me not to tell lies. You believed the wicked people who brought me here rather than myself. However, as you will not be friendly, I think we had better go. Come, Charlie?'

"'Don't go, princess,' pleaded little Eddie.

"'But I must, for your auntie does not like me,' said Chrissy.

"'I am sure I always meant to do my duty by you. And I will do so still.-- Beware, my dear young woman, of the deceitfulness of riches. Your carriage won't save your soul!'

"Chrissy was on the point of saying something rude, as she confessed when we got out; but she did not. She made her bow, turned and walked away. I followed, and poor Eddie would have done so too, but was laid hold of by his aunt. I confess this was not quite proper behaviour on Chrissy's part; but I never discovered that till she made me see it. She was very sorry afterwards, and my uncle feared the brougham had begun to hurt her already, as she told me. For she had narrated the whole story to him, and his look first let her see that she had been wrong. My uncle went with her afterwards to see Mrs. Sprinx, and thank her for having done her best; and to take Eddie such presents as my uncle only knew how to buy for children. When he went to school, I know he sent him a gold watch. From that time till now that she is my wife, Chrissy has had no more such adventures; and if Uncle Peter did not die on Christmas-day, it did not matter much, for Christmas-day makes all the days of the year as sacred as itself."

CHAPTER II.
THE GIANT'S HEART.

When Harry had finished reading, the colonel gallantly declared that the story was the best they had had. Mrs. Armstrong received this as a joke, and begged him not to be so unsparing.

"Ah! Mrs. Armstrong," returned he laughing, "you are not old enough yet, to know the truth from a joke. Don't you agree with me about the story, Mrs. Cathcart?"

"I think it is very pretty and romantic. Such men as Uncle Peter are not very common in the world. The story is not too true to Nature."

This she said in a tone intended to indicate superior acquaintance with the world and its nature. I fear Mrs. Cathcart and some others whom I could name, mean by ***Nature*** something very bad indeed, which yet an artist is bound to be loyal to. The colonel however seemed to be of a different opinion.

"If there never was such a man as Uncle Peter," said he, "there ought to have been; and it is all the more reason for putting him into a story that he is not to be found in the world."

"Bravo!" cried I. "You have answered a great question in a few words."

"I don't know," rejoined our host. "Have I? It seems to me as plain as the catechism."

I thought he might have found a more apt simile, but I held my peace.

Next morning, I walked out in the snow. Since the storm of that terrible night, it had fallen again quietly and plentifully; and now in the sunlight, the world--houses and trees, ponds and rivers--was like a creation, more than blocked out, but far from finished--in marble.

"And this," I said to myself, as I regarded the wondrous loveliness with which the snow had at once clothed and disfigured the bare branches of the trees, "this is what has come of the chaos of falling flakes! To this repose of beauty has that storm settled and sunk! Will it not be so with our mental storms as well?"

But here the figure displeased me; for those were not the true right shapes of the things; and the truth does not stick to things, but shows itself out of them.

"This lovely show," I said, "is the result of a busy fancy. This white world is the creation of a poet such as Shelley, in whom the fancy was too much for the intellect. Fancy settles upon anything; half destroys its form, half beautifies it with something that is not its own. But the true creative imagination, the form-seer, and the form-bestower, falls like the rain in the spring night, vanishing amid the roots of the trees; not settling upon them in clouds of wintry white, but breaking forth from them in clouds of summer green."

And then my thoughts very naturally went from Nature to my niece; and I asked myself whether within the last few days I had not seen upon her countenance the expression of a mental spring-time. For the mind has its seasons four, with many changes, as well as the world, only that the cycles are generally longer: they can hardly be more mingled than as here in our climate.

Let me confess, now that the subject of the confession no longer exists, that there had been something about Adela that, pet-child of mine as she was, had troubled me. In all her behaviour, so far as I had had any opportunity of judging, she had been as good as my desires at least. But there was a want in her face, a certain flatness of expression which I did not like. I love the common with all my heart, but I hate the common-place; and, foolish old bachelor that I am, the common-place in a woman troubles me, annoys me, makes me miserable. Well, it was something of the common-place in Adela's expression that had troubled me. Her eyes were clear, with lovely long dark lashes, but somehow the light in them had been always the same; and occasionally when I talked to her of the things I most wished her to care about, there was such an immobile condition of the features, associated with such a ready assent in words, that I felt her notion of what I meant must be something very different indeed from what I did mean. Her face looked as if it were made of something too thick for the inward light to shine through--wax, and not living muscle and skin. The fact was, the light within had not been kindled, else that face of hers would have been ready enough to let it shine out. Hitherto she had not seemed to me to belong at all to that company that praises God with sweet looks, as Thomas Hood describes Ruth as doing. What was wanting I had found it difficult to define. Her soul was asleep. She was dreaming a child's dreams, instead of seeing a woman's realities--realities that awake the swift play of feature, as the wind of God arouses the expression of a still landscape. So there seemed after all a gulf between her and me. She did not see what I saw, feel what I felt, seek what I sought. Occasionally even, the delicate young girl, pure and bright as the snow that hung on the boughs around me, would shock the wizened old bachelor with her worldliness--a worldliness that lay only in the use of current worldly phrases of selfish contentment, or selfish care. Ah! how little do young beauties understand of the pitiful emotions which they sometimes rouse in the breasts of men whom they suppose to be absorbed in admiration of them! But for faith that these girls are God's work and only half made yet, one would turn from them with sadness, almost painful dislike, and take refuge with some noble-faced grandmother, or withered old maid, whose features tell of sorrow and patience. And the beauty would think with herself that such a middle-aged gentleman did not admire pretty girls, and was severe and unkind and puritanical; whereas it was the lack of beauty that made him turn away; the disappointment of a face--dull, that ought to be radiant; or the presence of only that sort of beauty, which in middle age, except the deeper nature should meantime come into play, would be worse than common-place--would be mingled with the trail of more or less guilty sensuality. Many a woman at forty is repulsive, whom common men found at twenty irresistibly attractive; and many a woman at seventy is lovely to the eyes of the man who would have been compelled to allow that she was decidedly plain at seventeen.

"Maidens' bairns are aye weel guided," says the Scotch proverb; and the same may be said of bachelors' wives. So I will cease the strain, and return to Adela, the change in whom first roused it.

Of late, I had seen a glimmer of something in her countenance which I had never seen before--a something which, the first time I perceived it, made me say to her, in my own hearing only: "Ah, my dear, we shall understand each other by and by!" And now and then the light in her eye would be dimmed as by the foreshadowing of a tear, when there was no immediate and visible cause to account for it; and--which was very strange--I could not help fancying she began to be a little shy of her old uncle.--Could it be that she was afraid of his insight reaching to her heart, and reading there more than she was yet willing to confess to herself?--But whatever the cause of the change might be, there was certainly a responsiveness in her, a readiness to meet every utterance, and take it home, by which the vanity of the old bachelor would have been flattered to the full, had not his heart come first, and forestalled the delight.

So absorbed was I in considering these things, that the time passed like one of my thoughts; and before I knew I found myself on the verge of the perilous moor over which Harry had ridden in the teeth and heart of the storm. How smooth yet cruel it looked in its thick covering of snow! There was heather beneath, within which lay millions of purple bells, ready to rush out at the call of summer, and ring peals of merry gladness, making the desolate place not only blossom but rejoice as the rose. And there were cold wells of brown water beneath that snow, of depth unknown, which nourished nothing but the green grass that hid the cold glare of their presence from the eyes of the else warefully affrighted traveller. And I thought of Adela when I thought of the heather; and of some other woman whom I had known, when I thought of the wells.

When I came home, I told Adela where I had been, and what a desolate place it was. And the flush that rose on her pale cheek was just like the light of the sunset which I had left shining over the whiteness of that snowy region. And I said to myself: "It ***is*** so. And I trust it may be well."

As I walked home, I had bethought myself of a story which I had brought down with me in the hope of a chance of reading it, but which Adela's illness had put out of my mind; for it was only a child's story; and although I hoped older people might find something in it, it would have been absurd to read it without the presence of little children. So I said to Adela:

"Don't you know any little children in Purleybridge, Adela?"

"Oh! yes; plenty."

"Couldn't you ask some of them one night, and I would tell them a story. I think at this season they should have a share in what is going, and I have got one I think they would like."

"I shall be delighted. I will speak to papa about it at once. But next time--."

"Yes, I know. Next time Harry Armstrong was going to read; but to tell you the truth, Adela, I doubt if he will be ready. I know he is dreadfully busy just now, and I believe he will be thankful to have a reprieve for a day or two, and his story, which I expect will be a good one, will be all the better for it."

"Then I will speak to papa about it the moment he comes in; and you will tell Mr. Henry. And mind, uncle, you take the change upon your own shoulders."

"Trust me, my dear," I said, as I left the room.

As I had anticipated, Harry was grateful. Everything was arranged. So the next evening but one, we had a merry pretty company of boys and girls, none older, or at least looking older, than twelve. It did my heart good to see how Adela made herself at home with them, and talked to them as if she were one of themselves. By the time tea was over, I had made friends with them all, which was a stroke in its way nearly equal to Chaucer's, who made friends with all the nine and twenty Canterbury pilgrims before the sun was down. And the way I did was this. I began with the one next me, asking her the question:

"Do you like fairy-stories?"

"Yes, I do," answered she, heartily.

"Did you ever hear of the princess with the blue foot?"

"No. Will you tell me, please?"

Then I turned to the one on my other side, and asked her:

"Did you ever hear of the giant that was all skin--not skin and bone, you know, but all skin?"

"No-o" she answered, and her round blue eyes got rounder and bluer.

The next was a boy. I asked him:

"Did you ever hear of Don Worm of Wakemup?"

"No. Do please tell us about it."

And so I asked them, round the room. And by that time all eyes were fixed upon me. Then I said:

"You see I cannot tell you all these stories to-night. But would you all like one of some sort?"

A chorus of ***I should*** filled the room.

"What shall it be about, then?"

"A wicked fairy."

"No; that's stupid. I'm tired of wicked fairies," said a scornful little girl.

"A good giant, then," said a priggish imp, with a face as round as the late plum-pudding.

"I am afraid I could not tell you a story about a ***good*** giant; for unfortunately all the good giants I ever heard of were very stupid; so stupid that a story would not make itself about them; so stupid, indeed, that they were always made game of by creatures not half so big or half so good; and I don't like such stories. Shall I tell you about the wicked giant that grew little children in his garden instead of radishes, and then carried them about in his waistcoat pocket, and ate one as often as he remembered he had got some?"

"Yes, yes; please do."

"He used to catch little children and plant them in his garden, where you might see them in rows, with their heads only above ground, rolling their eyes about, and growing awfully fast. He liked greedy boys best--boys that ate plum-pudding till they felt as if their belts were too tight."

Here the fat-faced boy stuck both his hands inside his belt.

"Because he was so fond of radishes," I went on, "he lived just on the borders of Giantland, where it touched on the country of common people. Now, everything in Giantland was so big, that the common people saw only a mass of awful mountains and clouds; and no living man had ever come from it, as far as anybody knew, to tell what he had seen in it.

"Somewhere near these borders, on the other side, by the edge of a great forest, lived a labourer with his wife and a great many children. One day Tricksey-Wee, as they called her, teased her brother Buffy-Bob, till he could not bear it any longer, and gave her a box on the ear. Tricksey-Wee cried; and Buffy-Bob was so sorry and ashamed of himself, that he cried too, and ran off into the wood. He was so long gone, that Tricksey-Wee began to be frightened, for she was very fond of her brother; and she was so sorry that she had first teased him, and then cried, that at last she ran into the wood to look for him, though there was more chance of losing herself than of finding him. And, indeed, so it seemed likely to turn out; for, running on without looking, she at length found herself in a valley she knew nothing about. And no wonder; for what she thought was a valley with round, rocky sides, was no other than the space between two of the roots of a great tree that grew on the borders of Giantland. She climbed over the side of it, and right up to what she took for a black, round- topped mountain, far away; but she soon discovered that it was close to her, and was a hollow place so great that she could not tell what it was hollowed out of. Staring at it, she found that it was a doorway; and, going nearer and staring harder, she saw the door, far in, with a knocker of iron upon it, a great many yards above her head, and as large as the anchor of a big ship. Now, nobody had ever been unkind to Tricksey-Wee, and therefore she was not afraid of anybody. For Buffy-Bob's box on the ear she did not think worth considering. So, spying a little hole at the bottom of the door, which had been nibbled by some giant mouse, she crept through it, and found herself in an enormous hall, as big as if the late Mr. Martin, R.A., had been the architect. She could not have seen the other end of it at all, except for the great fire that was burning there, diminished to a spark in the distance. Towards this fire she ran as fast as she could, and was not far from it when something fell before her with a great clatter, over which she tumbled, and went rolling on the floor. She was not much hurt, however, and got up in a moment. Then she saw that she had fallen over something not unlike a great iron bucket. When she examined it more closely, she discovered that it was a thimble; and looking up to see who had dropped it, beheld a huge face, with spectacles as big as the round windows in a church, bending over her, and looking everywhere for the thimble. Tricksey-Wee immediately laid hold of it in both her arms, and lifted it about an inch nearer to the nose of the peering giantess. This movement made the old lady see where it was, and, her finger popping into it, it vanished from the eyes of Tricksey-Wee, buried in the folds of a white stocking, like a cloud in the sky, which Mrs. Giant was busy darning. For it was Saturday night, and her husband would wear nothing but white stockings on Sunday."

"But how could he be so particular about white stockings on Sunday, and eat little children?" asked one of the group.

"Why, to be sure," I answered, "he did eat little children, but only ***very*** little ones; and if ever it crossed his mind that it was wrong to do so, he always said to himself that he wore whiter stockings on Sunday than any other giant in all Giant-land.

"At that instant, Tricksey-Wee heard a sound like the wind in a tree full of leaves, and could not think what it could be; till, looking up, she found that it was the giantess whispering to her; and when she tried very hard, she could hear what she said well enough.

"'Run away, dear little girl,' she said, 'as fast as you can; for my husband will be home in a few minutes.'

"'But I've never been naughty to your husband,' said Tricksey-Wee, looking up in the giantess's face.

"'That doesn't matter. You had better go. He is fond of little children, particularly little girls!'

"'Oh! Then he won't hurt me.'

"'I am not sure of that. He is so fond of them that he eats them up; and I am afraid he couldn't help hurting you a little. He's a very good man though.'

"'Oh! then--' began Tricksey-Wee, feeling rather frightened; but before she could finish her sentence, she heard the sound of footsteps very far apart and very heavy. The next moment, who should come running towards her, full speed, and as pale as death, but Buffy-Bob! She held out her arms, and he ran into them. But when she tried to kiss him, she only kissed the back of his head; for his white face and round eyes were turned to the door.

"'Run, children; run and hide,' said the giantess.

"'Come, Buffy,' said Tricksey; 'yonder's a great brake; we'll hide in it.'

"The brake was a big broom; and they had just got into the bristles of it, when they heard the door open with a sound of thunder; and in stalked the giant. You would have thought you saw the whole earth through the door when he opened it, so wide was it; and, when he closed it, it was like nightfall.

"'Where is that little boy?' he cried, with a voice like the bellowing of cannon. 'He looked a very nice boy, indeed. I am almost sure he crept through the mouse hole at the bottom of the door. Where is he, my dear?'

"'I don't know,' answered the giantess.

"'But you know it is wicked to tell lies; don't you, dear?' retorted the giant.

"'Now, you ridiculous old Thunderthump!' said his wife, with a smile as broad as the sea in the sun; 'how can I mend your white stockings, and look after little boys? You have got plenty to last you over Sunday, I am sure. Just look what good little boys they are!'

"Tricksey-Wee and Buffy-Bob peered through the bristles, and discovered a row of little boys, about a dozen, with very fat faces and goggle eyes, sitting before the fire, and looking stupidly into it. Thunderthump intended the most of these for seed, and was feeding them well before planting them. Now and then, however, he could not keep his teeth off them, and would eat one by the bye, without salt."

* * * * *

"Now, you know that's all nonsense; for little children don't grow in gardens, I know. ***You*** may believe in the radish beds: ***I*** don't," said one pert little puss.

"I never said I did," replied I. "If the giant did, that's enough for my story. I told you the good giants are very stupid; so you may think what the bad ones are. Indeed, the giant never really tried the plan. No doubt he did plant the children, but he always pulled them up and ate them before they had a chance of increasing.

"He strode up to the wretched children. Now, what made them very wretched indeed was, that they knew if they could only keep from eating, and grow thin, the giant would dislike them, and turn them out to find their way home; but notwithstanding this, so greedy were they, that they ate as much as ever they could hold. The giantess, who fed them, comforted herself with thinking that they were not real boys and girls, but only little pigs pretending to be boys and girls.

"'Now tell me the truth,' cried the giant, bending his face down over them. They shook with terror, and every one hoped it was somebody else the giant liked best. 'Where is the little boy that ran into the hall just now? Whoever tells me a lie shall be instantly boiled.'

"'He's in the broom,' cried one dough-faced boy. 'He's in there, and a little girl with him.'

"'The naughty children,' cried the giant, 'to hide from ***me***!' And he made a stride towards the broom.

"'Catch hold of the bristles, Bobby. Get right into a tuft, and hold on,' cried Tricksey-Wee, just in time.

"The giant caught up the broom, and seeing nothing under it, set it down again with a bang that threw them both on the floor. He then made two strides to the boys, caught the dough-faced one by the neck, took the lid off a great pot that was boiling on the fire, popped him in as if he had been a trussed chicken, put the lid on again, and saying, 'There boys! See what comes of lying!' asked no more questions; for, as he always kept his word, he was afraid he might have to do the same to them all; and he did not like boiled boys. He like to eat them crisp, as radishes, whether forked or not, ought to be eaten. He then sat down, and asked his wife if his supper was ready. She looked into the pot, and, throwing the boy out with the ladle, as if he had been a black-beetle that had tumbled in and had had the worst of it, answered that she thought it was. Whereupon he rose to help her; and, taking the pot from the fire, poured the whole contents, bubbling and splashing into a dish like a vat. Then they say down to supper. The children in the broom could not see what they had; but it seemed to agree with them; for the giant talked like thunder, and the giantess answered like the sea, and they grew chattier and chattier. At length the giant said:

"'I don't feel quite comfortable about that heart of mine.' And as he spoke, instead of laying his hand on his bosom, he waved it away towards the corner where the children were peeping from the broom-bristles, like frightened little mice.

"'Well, you know, my darling Thunderthump,' answered his wife, 'I always thought it ought to be nearer home. But you know best, of course.'

"'Ha! ha! You don't know where it is, wife. I moved it a month ago.'

"'What a man you are, Thunderthump! You trust any creature alive rather than your wife.'

"Here the giantess gave a sob which sounded exactly like a wave going flop into the mouth of a cave up to the roof.

"'Where have you got it now?' she resumed, checking her emotion.

"'Well, Doodlem, I don't mind telling ***you***,' said the giant, soothingly. 'The great she-eagle has got it for a nest-egg. She sits on it night and day, and thinks she will bring the greatest eagle out of it that ever sharpened his beak on the rocks of Mount Skycrack. I can warrant no one else will touch it while she has got it. But she is rather capricious, and I confess I am not easy about it; for the least scratch of one of her claws would do for me at once. And she ***has*** claws.'"

* * * * *

"What funny things you do make up!" said a boy. "How could the giant's heart be in an eagle's nest, and the giant himself alive and well without it?"

"Whatever you may think of it, Master Fred, I assure you I did not make it up.

If it ever was made up, no one can tell who did it; for it was written in the chronicles of Giantland long before one of us was born. It was quite common," said I, in an injured tone, "for a giant to put his heart out to nurse, because he did not like the trouble and responsibility of doing it himself. It was, I confess, a dangerous sort of thing to do.--But do you want any more of my story or not?"

"Oh! yes, please," cried Frederick, very heartily.

"Then don't you find any more fault with it, or I will stop."

Master Fred was straightway silent, and I went on.

* * * * *

"All this time Buffy-Bob and Tricksey-Wee were listening with long ears. ***They*** did not dispute about the giant's heart, and impossibility, and all that; for they were better educated than Master Fred, and knew all about it. 'Oh!' thought Tricksey-Wee, 'if I could but find the giant's cruel heart, wouldn't I give it a squeeze!'

"The giant and giantess went on talking for a long time. The giantess kept advising the giant to hide his heart somewhere in the house; but he seemed afraid of the advantage it would give her over him.

"'You could hide it at the bottom of the flour-barrel,' said she.

"'That would make me feel chokey,' answered he.

"'Well, in the coal-cellar, or in the dust-hole. That's the place! No one would think of looking for your heart in the dust-hole.'

"'Worse and worse!' cried the giant.

"'Well, the water-butt?' said she.

"'No, no; it would grow spongy there,' said he.

"'Well, what will you do with it?'

"'I will leave it a month longer where it is, and then I will give it to the Queen of the Kangaroos, and she will carry it in her pouch for me. It is best to change, you know, and then my enemies can't find it. But, dear Doodlem, it's a fretting care to have a heart of one's own to look after. The responsibility is too much for me. If it were not for a bite of a radish now and then, I never could bear it.'

"Here the giant looked lovingly towards the row of little boys by the fire, all of whom were nodding, or asleep on the floor.

"'Why don't you trust it to me, dear Thunderthump?' said his wife. 'I would take the best possible care of it.'

"'I don't doubt it, my love. But the responsibility would be too much for you. You would no longer be my darling, light-hearted, airy, laughing Doodlem. It would transform you into a heavy, oppressed woman, weary of life--as I am.'

"The giant closed his eyes and pretended to go to sleep. His wife got his stockings, and went on with her darning. Soon, the giant's pretence became reality, and the giantess began to nod over her work.

"'Now, Buffy,' whispered Tricksey-Wee, 'now's our time. I think it's moonlight, and we had better be off. There's a door with a hole for the cat just behind us.'

"'All right!' said Bob; 'I'm ready.'

"So they got out of the broom-brake, and crept to the door. But, to their great disappointment, when they got through it, they found themselves in a sort of shed. It was full of tubs and things, and, though it was built of wood only, they could not find a crack.

"'Let us try this hole,' said Tricksey; for the giant and giantess were sleeping behind them, and they dared not go back.

"'All right,' said Bob. He seldom said anything else than ***All right***.

"Now this hole was in a mound that came in through the wall of the shed and went along the floor for some distance. They crawled into it, and found it very dark. But groping their way along, they soon came to a small crack, through which they saw grass, pale in the moonshine. As they crept on, they found the hole began to get wider and lead upwards.

"'What is that noise of rushing?' said Buffy-Bob.

"'I can't tell,' replied Tricksey; 'for, you see, I don't know what we are in.'

"The fact was, they were creeping along a channel in the heart of a giant tree; and the noise they heard was the noise of the sap rushing along in its wooden pipes. When they laid their ears to the wall, they heard it gurgling along with a pleasant noise.

"'It sounds kind and good,' said Tricksey. 'It is water running. Now it must be running from somewhere to somewhere. I think we had better go on, and we shall come somewhere.'

"It was now rather difficult to go on, for they had to climb as if they were climbing a hill; and now the passage was wide. Nearly worn out, they saw light overhead at last, and creeping through a crack into the open air, found themselves on the fork of a huge tree. A great, broad, uneven space lay around them, out of which spread boughs in every direction, the smallest of them as big as the biggest tree in the country of common people. Overhead were leaves enough to supply all the trees they had ever seen. Not much moonlight could come through, but the leaves would glimmer white in the wind at times. The tree was full of giant birds. Every now and then, one would sweep through, with a great noise. But, except an occasional chirp, sounding like a shrill pipe in a great organ, they made no noise. All at once an owl began to hoot. He thought he was singing. As soon as he began, other birds replied, making rare game of him. To their astonishment, the children found they could understand every word they sang. And what they said was something like this:

"'I will sing a song.
 I'm the owl.'
'Sing a song, you sing-song
 Ugly fowl!
What will you sing about,
 Now the light is out?'

"'Sing about the night;
 I'm the owl.'
'You could not see for the light,
 Stupid fowl.'
'Oh! the moon! and the dew!
 And the shadows!--tu-whoo!'

"The owl spread out his silent, soft, sly wings, and lighting between Tricksey-Wee and Buffy-Bob, nearly smothered them, closing up one under each wing. It was like being buried in a down bed. But the owl did not like anything between his sides and his wings, so he opened his wings again, and the children made haste to get out. Tricksey-Wee immediately went in front of the bird, and looking up into his huge face, which was as round as the eyes of the giantess's spectacles, and much bigger, dropped a pretty courtesy, and said:

"'Please, Mr. Owl, I want to whisper to you.'

"'Very well, small child,' answered the owl, looking important, and stooping his ear towards her. 'What is it?'

"'Please tell me where the eagle lives that sits on the giant's heart.'

"'Oh, you naughty child! That's a secret. For shame!'

"And with a great hiss that terrified them, the owl flew into the tree. All birds are fond of secrets; but not many of them can keep them so well as the owl.

"So the children went on because they did not know what else to do. They found the way very rough and difficult, the tree was so full of humps and hollows. Now and then they plashed into a pool of rain; now and then they came upon twigs growing out of the trunk where they had no business, and they were as large as full-grown poplars. Sometimes they came upon great cushions of soft moss, and on one of them they lay down and rested. But they had not lain long before they spied a large nightingale sitting on a branch, with its bright eyes looking up at the moon. In a moment more he began to sing, and the birds about him began to reply, but in a very different tone from that in which they had replied to the owl. Oh, the birds did call the nightingale such pretty names! The nightingale sang, and the birds replied like this:--

"I will sing a song.
  I'm the nightingale.'
'Sing a song, long, long,
  Little Neverfail!
What will you sing about,
  Light in or light out?'

'Sing about the light
  Gone away;
Down, away, and out of sight--
  Poor lost day!

Mourning for the day dead,
O'er his dim bed.'

"The nightingale sang so sweetly, that the children would have fallen asleep but for fear of losing any of the song. When the nightingale stopped they got up and wandered on. They did not know where they were going, but they thought it best to keep going on, because then they might come upon something or other. They were very sorry they forgot to ask the nightingale about the eagle's nest, but his music had put everything else out of their heads. They resolved, however, not to forget the next time they had a chance. They went on and on, till they were both tired, and Tricksey-Wee said at last, trying to laugh,

"'I declare my legs feel just like a Dutch doll's.'

"'Then here's the place to go to bed in,' said Buffy-Bob.

"They stood at the edge of a last year's nest, and looked down with delight into the round, mossy cave. Then they crept gently in, and, lying down in each other's arms, found it so deep, and warm, and comfortable, and soft, that they were soon fast asleep.

"Now close beside them, in a hollow, was another nest, in which lay a lark and his wife; and the children were awakened very early in the morning, by a dispute between Mr. and Mrs. Lark.

"'Let me up,' said the lark.

"'It is not time,' said the lark's wife.

"'It is,' said the lark, rather rudely. 'The darkness is quite thin. I can almost see my own beak.'

"'Nonsense!' said the lark's wife. 'You know you came home yesterday morning quite worn out--you had to fly so very high before you saw him. I am sure he would not mind if you took it a little easier. Do be quiet and go to sleep again.'

"'That's not it at all,' said the lark. 'He doesn't want me. I want him. Let me up, I say.'

"He began to sing; and Tricksey-Wee and Buffy-Bob, having now learned the way, answered him:--

"'I will sing a song,
I'm the Lark.'
'Sing, sing, Throat-strong,
Little Kill-the-dark.
What will you sing about,
Now the night is out?'

"'I can only call;
I can't think.
Let me up--that's all.
Let me drink!
Thirsting all the long night
For a drink of light.'

"By this time the lark was standing on the edge of his nest and looking at the children.

"'Poor little things! You can't fly,' said the lark.

"'No; but we can look up,' said Tricksey.

"'Ah! you don't know what it is to see the very first of the sun.'

"'But we know what it is to wait till he comes. He's no worse for your seeing him first, is he?'

"'Oh! no, certainly not,' answered the lark, with condescension; and then, bursting into his ***jubilate***, he sprung aloft, clapping his wings like a clock running down.

"'Tell us where--' began Buffy-Bob.

"But the lark was out of sight. His song was all that was left of him. That was everywhere, and he was nowhere.

"'Selfish bird!' said Buffy. 'It's all very well for larks to go hunting the sun, but they have no business to despise their neighbours, for all that.'

"'Can I be of any use to you?' said a sweet bird-voice out of the nest. This was the lark's wife, who staid at home with the young larks while her husband went to church.

"'Oh! thank you. If you please,' answered Tricksey-Wee.

"And up popped a pretty brown head; and then up came a brown feathery body; and last of all came the slender legs on to the edge of the nest. There she turned, and, looking down into the nest, from which came a whole litany of chirpings for breakfast, said, 'Lie still, little ones.' Then she turned to the children. 'My husband is King of the Larks,' she said.

"Buffy-Bob took off his cap, and Tricksey-Wee courtesied very low.

"'Oh, it's not me,' said the bird, looking very shy. 'I am only his wife. It's my husband.' And she looked up after him into the sky, whence his song was still falling like a shower of musical hailstones. Perhaps she could see him.

"'He's a splendid bird,' said Buffy-Bob; 'only you know he ***will*** get up a little too early.'

"'Oh, no! he doesn't. It's only his way, you know. But tell me what I can do for you.'

"'Tell us, please, Lady Lark, where the she-eagle lives that sits on Giant Thunderthump's heart.'

"'Oh! that is a secret.'

"'Did you promise not to tell?'

"'No; but larks ought to be discreet. They see more than other birds.'

"'But you don't fly up high like your husband, do you?'

"'Not often. But it's no matter. I come to know things for all that.'

"'Do tell me, and I will sing you a song,' said Tricksey-Wee.

"'Can you sing too?'

"'Yes. And I will sing you a song I learned the other day about a lark and his wife.'

"'Please do,' said the lark's wife. 'Be quiet, children, and listen.'

"Tricksey-Wee was very glad she happened to know a song which would please the lark's wife, at least, whatever the lark himself might have thought of it, if he had heard it. So she sang:

"'Good morrow, my lord!' in the sky alone, Sang the lark, as the sun ascended his throne. 'Shine on me, my lord; I only am come, Of all your servants, to welcome you home. I have flown for an hour, right up, I swear, To catch the first shine of your golden hair!'

'Must I thank you, then,' said the king, 'Sir Lark, For flying so high, and hat-ing the dark? You ask a full cup for half a thirst: Half is love of me, and half love to be first. There's many a bird that makes no haste, But waits till I come. That's as much to my taste.'

And the king hid his head in a turban of cloud; And the lark stopped singing, quite vexed and cowed. But he flew up higher, and thought, 'Anon, The wrath of the king will be over and gone; And his crown, shining out of the cloudy fold, Will change my brown feathers to a glory of gold.'

So he flew, with the strength of a lark he flew. But, as he rose, the cloud rose too; And not a gleam of the golden hair Came through the depth of the misty air; Till, weary with flying, with sighing sore, The strong sun-seeker could do no more.

His wings had had no chrism of gold; And his feathers felt withered and worn and old; And he sank, and quivered, and dropped like a stone. And there on his nest, where he left her, alone, Sat his little wife on her little eggs, Keeping them warm with wings and legs.

Did I say alone? Ah, no such thing! Full in her face was shining the king. 'Welcome, Sir Lark! You look tired,' said he. 'Up is not always the best way to me. While you have been singing so high and away, I've been shining to your little wife all day.'

He had set his crown all about the nest, And out of the midst shone her little brown breast; And so glorious was she in russet gold, That for wonder and awe Sir Lark grew cold. He popped his head under her wing, and lay As still as a stone, till the king was away.

"As soon as Tricksey-Wee had finished her song, the lark's wife began a low, sweet, modest little song of her own; and after she had piped away for two or three minutes, she said:

"'You dear children, what can I do for you?'

"'Tell us where the she-eagle lives, please,' said Tricksey-Wee.

"'Well, I don't think there can be much harm in telling such wise, good children,' said Lady Lark; 'I am sure you don't want to do any mischief.'

"'Oh, no; quite the contrary,' said Buffy-Bob.

"'Then I'll tell you. She lives on the very topmost peak of Mount Skycrack; and the only way to get up is, to climb on the spiders' webs that cover it from top to bottom.'

"'That's rather serious,' said Tricksey-Wee.

"'But you don't want to go up, you foolish little thing. You can't go. And what do you want to go up for?'

"'That is a secret,' said Tricksey-Wee.

"'Well, it's no business of mine,' rejoined Lady Lark, a little offended, and quite vexed that she had told them. So she flew away to find some breakfast for her little ones, who by this time were chirping very impatiently. The children looked at each other, joined hands, and walked off.

"In a minute more the sun was up, and they soon reached the outside of the tree. The bark was so knobby and rough, and full of twigs, that they managed to get down, though not without great difficulty. Then, far away to the north, they saw a huge peak, like the spire of a church, going right up into the sky. They thought this must be Mount Skycrack, and turned their faces towards it. As they went on, they saw a giant or two, now and then, striding about the fields or through the woods, but they kept out of their way. Nor were they in much danger; for it was only one or two of the border giants that were so very fond of children. At last they came to the foot of Mount Skycrack. It stood in a plain alone, and shot right up, I don't know how many thousand feet, into the air, a long, narrow, spearlike mountain. The whole face of it, from top to bottom, was covered with a network of spiders' webs, with threads of various sizes, from that of silk to that of whipcord. The webs shook, and quivered, and waved in the sun, glittering like silver. All about ran huge, greedy spiders, catching huge, silly flies, and devouring them.

"Here they sat down to consider what could be done. The spiders did not heed them, but ate away at the flies. At the foot of the mountain, and all round it, was a ring of water, not very broad, but very deep. Now, as they sat watching, one of the spiders, whose web was woven across this water, somehow or other lost his hold, and fell on his back. Tricksey-Wee and Buffy-Bob ran to his assistance, and laying hold each of one of his legs, succeeded, with the help of the other legs, which struggled spiderfully, in getting him out upon dry land. As soon as he had shaken himself, and dried himself a little, the spider turned to the children, saying,

"'And now, what can I do for you?'

"'Tell us, please,' said they, 'how we can get up the mountain to the she-eagle's nest.'

"'Nothing is easier,' answered the spider. 'Just run up there, and tell them all I sent you, and nobody will mind you.'

"'But we haven't got claws like you, Mr. Spider,' said Buffy.

"'Ah! no more you have, poor unprovided creatures! Still, I think we can manage it. Come home with me.'

"'You won't eat us, will you?' said Buffy.

"'My dear child,' answered the spider, in a tone of injured dignity, 'I eat nothing but what is mischievous or useless. You have helped me, and now I will help you.'

"The children rose at once, and, climbing as well as they could, reached the spider's nest in the centre of the web. They did not find it very difficult; for whenever too great a gap came, the spider spinning a strong cord stretched it just where they would have chosen to put their feet next. He left them in his nest, after bringing them two enormous honey-bags, taken from bees that he had caught. Presently about six of the wisest of the spiders came back with him. It was rather horrible to look up and see them all round the mouth of the nest, looking down on them in contemplation, as if wondering whether they would be nice eating. At length one of them said:

"'Tell us truly what you want with the eagle, and we will try to help you.'

"Then Tricksey-Wee told them that there was a giant on the borders who treated little children no better than radishes, and that they had narrowly escaped being eaten by him; that they had found out that the great she-eagle of Mount Skycrack was at present sitting on his heart; and that, if they could only get hold of the heart, they would soon teach the giant better behaviour.

"'But,' said their host, 'if you get at the heart of the giant, you will find it as large as one of your elephants. What can you do with it?'

"'The least scratch will kill it,' answered Buffy-Bob.

"'Ah! but you might do better than that,' said the spider.--'Now we have resolved to help you. Here is a little bag of spider-juice. The giants cannot bear spiders, and this juice is dreadful poison to them. We are all ready to go up with you, and drive the eagle away. Then you must put the heart into this other bag, and bring it down with you; for then the giant will be in your power.'

"'But how can we do that?' said Buffy. 'The bag is not much bigger than a pudding-bag.'

"'But it is as large as you will find convenient to carry.'

"'Yes; but what are we to do with the heart?'

"'Put it into the bag, to be sure. Only, first, you must squeeze a drop out of the other bag upon it. You will see what will happen.'

"'Very well; we will,' said Tricksey-Wee. 'And now, if you please, how shall we go?'

"'Oh, that's our business,' said the first spider. 'You come with me, and my grandfather will take your brother. Get up.'

"So Tricksey-Wee mounted on the narrow part of the spider's back, and held fast. And Buffy-Bob got on the grandfather's back. And up they scrambled, over one web after another, up and up. And every spider followed; so that, when Tricksey-Wee looked back, she saw a whole army of spiders scrambling after them.

"'What can we want with so many?' she thought; but she said nothing.

"The moon was now up, and it was a splendid sight below and around them. All Giantland was spread out under them, with its great hills, lakes, trees, and animals. And all above them was the clear heaven, and Mount Skycrack rising into it, with its endless ladders of spiderwebs, glittering like cords made of moonbeams. And up the moonbeams went, crawling, and scrambling, and racing, a huge army of huge spiders.

"At length they reached all but the very summit, where they stopped. Tricksey-Wee and Buffy-Bob could see above them a great globe of feathers, that finished off the mountain like an ornamental knob.

"'How shall we drive her off?' said Buffy.

"'We'll soon manage that,' said the grandfather spider. 'Come on, you, down there.'

"Up rushed the whole army, past the children, over the edge of the nest, on to the she-eagle, and buried themselves in her feathers. In a moment she became very restless, and went picking about with her beak. All at once she spread out her wings, with a sound like a whirlwind, and flew off to bathe in the sea; and then the spiders began to drop from her in all directions on their gossamer wings. The children had to hold fast to keep the wind of the eagle's flight from blowing them off.

As soon as it was over, they looked into the nest, and there lay the giant's heart--an awful and ugly thing.

"'Make haste, child!' said Tricksey's spider. So Tricksey took her bag, and squeezed a drop out of it upon the heart. She thought she heard the giant give a far-off roar of pain, and she nearly fell from her seat with terror. The heart instantly began to shrink. It shrunk and shrivelled till it was nearly gone; and Buffy-Bob caught it up and put it into the bag. Then the two spiders turned and went down again as fast as they could. Before they got to the bottom, they heard the shrieks of the she-eagle over the loss of her egg; but the spiders told them not to be alarmed, for her eyes were too big to see them. By the time they reached the foot of the mountain, all the spiders had got home, and were busy again catching flies, as if nothing had happened. So the children, after renewed thanks to their friends, set off, carrying the giant's heart with them.

"'If you should find it at all troublesome, just give it a little more spider-juice directly,' said the grandfather, as they took their leave.

"Now, the giant had given an awful roar of pain, the moment they anointed his heart, and had fallen down in a fit, in which he lay so long that all the boys might have escaped if they had not been so fat. One did--and got home in safety. For days the giant was unable to speak. The first words he uttered were,

"'Oh, my heart! my heart!'

"'Your heart is safe enough, dear Thunderthump,' said his wife. 'Really a man of your size ought not to be so nervous and apprehensive. I am ashamed of you.'

"'You have no heart, Doodlem,' answered he. 'I assure you that this moment mine is in the greatest danger. It has fallen into the hands of foes, though who they are I cannot tell.'

"Here he fainted again; for Tricksey-Wee, finding the heart begin to swell a little, had given it the least touch of spider-juice.

"Again he recovered, and said:

"'Dear Doodlem, my heart is coming back to me. It is coming nearer and nearer.'

"After lying silent for a few hours, he exclaimed:

"'It is in the house, I know!' And he jumped up and walked about, looking in every corner.

"Just then, Tricksey-Wee and Buffy-Bob came out of the hole in the tree-root, and through the cat-hole in the door, and walked boldly towards the giant. Both kept their eyes busy watching him. Led by the love of his own heart, the giant soon spied them, and staggered furiously towards them.

"'I will eat you, you vermin!' he cried. 'Give me my heart.'

"Tricksey gave the heart a sharp pinch; when down fell the giant on his knees, blubbering, and crying, and begging for his heart.

"'You shall have it, if you behave yourself properly,' said Tricksey.

"'What do you want me to do?' asked he, whimpering.

"'To take all those boys and girls, and carry them home at once.'

"'I'm not able; I'm too ill.'

"'Take them up directly.'

"'I can't, till you give me my heart.'

"'Very well!' said Tricksey; and she gave the heart another pinch.

"The giant jumped to his feet, and catching up all the children, thrust some into his waistcoat pockets, some into his breast-pocket, put two or three into his hat, and took a bundle of them under each arm. Then he staggered to the door. All this time poor Doodlem was sitting in her armchair, crying, and mending a white stocking.

"The giant led the way to the borders. He could not go fast, so that Buffy and Tricksey managed to keep up with him. When they reached the borders, they thought it would be safer to let the children find their own way home. So they told him to set them down. He obeyed.

"'Have you put them all down, Mr. Thunderthump?' asked. Tricksey-Wee.

"'Yes,' said the giant.

"'That's a lie!' squeaked a little voice; and out came a head from his waistcoat-pocket.

"Tricksey-Wee pinched the heart till the giant roared with pain.

"'You're not a gentleman. You tell stories,' she said.

"'He was the thinnest of the lot,' said Thunderthump, crying.

"'Are you all there now, children?' asked Tricksey.

"'Yes, ma'am,' said they, after counting themselves very carefully, and with some difficulty; for they were all stupid children.

"'Now,' said Tricksey-Wee to the giant, 'will you promise to carry off no more children, and never to eat a child again all you life?'

"'Yes, yes! I promise,' answered Thunderthump, sobbing.

"'And you will never cross the borders of Giantland?'

"'Never.'

"'And you shall never again wear white stockings on a Sunday, all your life long.--Do you promise?'

"The giant hesitated at this, and began to expostulate; but Tricksey-Wee, believing it would be good for his morals, insisted; and the giant promised.

"Then she required of him, that, when she gave him back his heart, he should give it to his wife to take care of for him for ever after. The poor giant feel on his knees and began again to beg. But Tricksey-Wee giving the heart a slight pinch, he bawled out:

"'Yes, yes! Doodlem shall have it, I swear. Only she must not put it in the flour-barrel, or in the dust-hole.'

"'Certainly not. Make your own bargain with her.--And you promise not to interfere with my brother and me, or to take any revenge for what we have done?'

"'Yes, yes, my dear children; I promise everything. Do, pray, make haste and give me back my poor heart.'

"'Wait there, then, till I bring it to you.'

"'Yes, yes. Only make haste, for I feel very faint.'

"Tricksey-Wee began to undo the mouth of the bag. But Buffy-Bob, who had got very knowing on his travels, took out his knife with the pretence of cutting the string; but, in reality, to be prepared for any emergency.

"No sooner was the heart out of the bag, than it expanded to the size of a bullock; and the giant, with a yell of rage and vengeance, rushed on the two children, who had stepped sideways from the terrible heart. But Buffy-Bob was too quick for Thunderthump. He sprang to the heart, and buried his knife in it, up to the hilt. A fountain of blood spouted from it; and with a dreadful groan, the giant fell dead at the feet of little Tricksey-Wee, who could not help being sorry for him after all."

* * * * *

"Silly thing!" said a little wisehead.

"What a horrid story!" said one small girl with great eyes, who sat staring into the fire.

"I don't think it at all a nice story for supper, with those horrid spiders, too," said an older girl.

"Well, let us have a game and forget it," I said.

"No; that we shan't, I am sure," said one.

"I will tell our Amy. Won't it be fun?"

"She'll scream," said another.

"I'll tell her all the more."

"No, no; you mustn't be unkind," said I; "else you will never help little children against wicked giants. The giants will eat you too, then."

"Oh! I know what you mean. You can't frighten me."

This was said by one of the elder girls, who promised fair to reach before long the summit of uncompromising womanhood. She made me feel very small with my moralizing; so I dropt it. On the whole I was rather disappointed with the effect of my story. Perhaps the disappointment was no more than I deserved; but I did not like to think I had failed with children.

Nor did I think so any longer after a darling little blue-eyed girl, who had sat next me at tea, came to me to say good night, and, reaching up, put her arms round my neck and kissed me, and then whispered very gently:

"Thank you, dear Mr. Smith. I will be good. It was a very nice story. If I was a man, I would kill all the wicked people in the world. But I am only a little girl, you know; so I can only be good."

The darling did not know how much more one good woman can do to kill evil than all the swords of the world in the hands of righteous heroes.

CHAPTER III.
A CHILD'S HOLIDAY.

When the next evening of our assembly came, I could see on Adela's face a look of subdued expectation, and I knew now to what to attribute it: Harry was going to read. There was a restlessness in her eyelids--they were always rising, and falling as suddenly. But when the time drew near, they grew more still; only her colour went and came a little. By the time we were all seated, she was as quiet as death. Harry pulled out a manuscript.

"Have you any objection to a ballad-story?" he asked of the company generally.

"Certainly not," was the common reply; though Ralph stared a little, and his wife looked at him. I believe the reason was, that they had never known Harry write poetry before. But as soon as he had uttered the title-- "The Two Gordons"--

"You young rascal!" cried his brother. "Am I to keep you in material for ever? Are you going to pluck my wings till they are as bare as an egg? Really, ladies and gentlemen," he continued, in pretended anger, while Harry was keeping down a laugh of keen enjoyment, "it is too bad of that scapegrace brother of mine! Of course you are all welcome to anything I have got; but he has no right to escape from his responsibilities on that account. It is rude to us all. I know he can write if he likes."

"Why, Ralph, you would be glad of such a brother to steal your sermons from, if you had been up all night as I was. Of course I did not mean to claim any more credit than that of unearthing some of your shy verses.-- May I read them or not?"

"Oh! of course. But it is lucky I came prepared for some escapade of the sort, and brought a manuscript of proper weight and length in my pocket."

Suddenly Harry's face changed from a laughing to a grave one. I saw how it was. He had glanced at Adela, and her look of unmistakeable disappointment was reflected in his face. But there was a glimmer of pleasure in his eyes, notwithstanding; and I fancied I could see that the pleasure would have been more marked, had he not feared that he had placed himself at a disadvantage with her, namely, that she would suppose him incapable of producing a story. However, it was only for a moment that this change of feeling stopped him. With a gesture of some haste he re-opened the manuscript, which he had rolled up as if to protect it from the indignation of his brother, and read the following ballad:

"The Two Gordons.

I

"There was John Gordon, and Archibold,
   And an earl's twin sons were they.
When they were one and twenty years old,
   They fell out on their birth-day.

"'Turn,' said Archibold, 'brother sly!
   Turn now, false and fell;
Or down thou goest, as black as a lie,
   To the father of lies in hell.'

"'Why this to me, brother Archie, I pray?
   What ill have I done to thee?'
'Smooth-faced hound, thou shall rue the day
   Thou gettest an answer of me.

"'For mine will be louder than Lady Janet's,
   And spoken in broad daylight--
And the wall to scale is my iron mail,
   Not her castle wall at night.'

"'I clomb the wall of her castle tall,
In the moon and the roaring wind;
It was dark and still in her bower until
The morning looked in behind.'

"'Turn therefore, John Gordon, false brother;
For either thou or I,
On a hard wet bed--wet, cold, and red,
For evermore shall lie.'

"'Oh, Archibold, Janet is my true love;
Would I had told it thee!'
'I hate thee the worse. Turn, or I'll curse
The night that got thee and me.'

"Their swords they drew, and the sparks they flew,
As if hammers did anvils beat;
And the red blood ran, till the ground began
To plash beneath their feet.

"'Oh, Archie! thou hast given me a cold supper,
A supper of steel, I trow;
But reach me one grasp of a brother's hand,
And turn me, before you go.'

"But he turned himself on his gold-spurred heel,
And away, with a speechless frown;
And up in the oak, with a greedy croak,
The carrion-crow claimed his own.

II

"The sun looked over a cloud of gold;
Lady Margaret looked over the wall.
Over the bridge rode Archibold;
Behind him his merry men all.

"He leads his band to the holy land.
They follow with merry din.
A white Christ's cross is on his back;
In his breast a darksome sin.

"And the white cross burned him like the fire,
That he could nor eat nor rest;
It burned in and in, to get at the sin,
That lay cowering in his breast.

"A mile from the shore of the Dead Sea,
The army lay one night.
Lord Archibold rose; and out he goes,
Walking in the moonlight.

"He came to the shore of the old salt sea--
Yellow sands with frost-like tinge;
The bones of the dead on the edge of its bed,
Lay lapped in its oozy fringe.

"He sat him down on a half-sunk stone,
And he sighed so dreary and deep:
'The devil may take my soul when I wake,
If he'd only let me sleep!'

"Out from the bones and the slime and the stones,
Came a voice like a raven's croak:
'Was it thou, Lord Archibold Gordon?' it said,
'Was it thou those words that spoke?'

"'I'll say them again,' quoth Archibold,
'Be thou ghost or fiend of the deep.'
'Lord Archibold heed how thou may'st speed,
If thou sell me thy soul for sleep.'

"Lord Archibold laughed with a loud _ha! ha!_--
The Dead Sea curdled to hear:
'Thou would'st have the worst of the bargain curst--
It has every fault but fear.'

"'Done, Lord Archibold?' 'Lord Belzebub, done!'
His laugh came back in a moan.
The salt glittered on, and the white moon shone,
And Lord Archibold was alone.

"And back he went to his glimmering tent;
And down in his cloak he lay;
And sound he slept; and a pale-faced man
Watched by his bed till day.

"And if ever he turned or moaned in his sleep,
Or his brow began to lower,
Oh! gentle and clear, in the sleeper's ear,
He would whisper words of power;

"Till his lips would quiver, and sighs of bliss
From sorrow's bosom would break;
And the tear, soft and slow, would gather and flow;

And yet he would not wake.

"Every night the pale-faced man
Sat by his bed, I say;
And in mail rust-brown, with his visor down,
Rode beside him in battle-fray.

"But well I wot that it was not
The devil that took his part;
But his twin-brother John, he thought dead and gone,
Who followed to ease his heart.

III

"Home came Lord Archibold, weary wight,
Home to his own countree;
And he cried, when his castle came in sight,
'Now Christ me save and see!'

"And the man in rust-brown, with his visor down,
Had gone, he knew not where.
And he lighted down, and into the hall,
And his mother met him there.

"But dull was her eye, though her mien was high;
And she spoke like Eve to Cain:
'Lord Archibold Gordon, answer me true,
Or I'll never speak again.

"'Where is thy brother, Lord Archibold?
He was flesh and blood of thine.
Has thy brother's keeper laid him cold,
Where the warm sun cannot shine?'

"Lord Archibold could not speak a word,
For his heart was almost broke.
He turned to go. The carrion-crow
At the window gave a croak.

"'Now where art thou going, Lord Archie?' she said,
'With thy lips so white and thin?'
'Mother, good-bye; I am going to lie
In the earth with my brother-twin.'

"Lady Margaret sank on her couch. 'Alas!
I shall lose them both to-day.'
Lord Archibold strode along the road,
To the field of the Brothers' Fray.

"He came to the spot where they had fought.
'My God!' he cried in fright,
'They have left him there, till his bones are bare;
Through the plates they glimmer white.'

"For his brother's armour lay there, dank,
And worn with frost and dew.
Had the long, long grass that grew so rank,
Grown the very armour through?

"'O brother, brother!' cried the Earl,
With a loud, heart-broken wail,
'I would put my soul into thy bones,
To see thee alive and hale.'

"'Ha! ha!' said a voice from out the helm--
'Twas the voice of the Dead Sea shore--
And the joints did close, and the armour rose,

And clattered and grass uptore--

"'Thou canst put no soul into his bones,
Thy brother alive to set;
For the sleep was thine, and thy soul is mine,
And, Lord Archibold, well-met!'

"'Two words to that!' said the fearless Earl;
'The sleep was none of thine;
For I dreamed of my brother all the night--
His soul brought the sleep to mine.

"'But I care not a crack for a soul so black,
And thou may'st have it yet:
I would let it burn to eternity,
My brother alive to set.'

"The demon lifted his beaver up,
Crusted with blood and mould;
And, lo! John Gordon looked out of the helm,
And smiled upon Archibold.

"'Thy soul is mine, brother Archie,' he said,
'And I yield it thee none the worse;
No devil came near thee, Archie, lad,
But a brother to be thy nurse.'

"Lord Archibold fell upon his knee,
On the blood-fed, bright green sod:
'The soul that my brother gives back to me,
Is thine for ever, O God!'"

"Now for a piece of good, honest prose!" said the curate, the moment Harry had finished, without allowing room for any remarks. "That is, if the ladies and gentlemen will allow me to read once more."

Of course, all assented heartily.

"It is nothing of a story, but I think it is something of a picture, drawn principally from experiences of my own childhood, which I told you was spent chiefly in the north of Scotland. The one great joy of the year, although some years went without it altogether, was the summer visit paid to the shores of the Moray Firth. My story is merely a record of some of the impressions left on myself by such a visit, although the boy is certainly not a portrait of myself; and if it has no result, no end, reaching beyond childhood into what is commonly called life, I presume it is not of a peculiar or solitary character in that respect; for surely many that we count finished stories--life-histories--must look very different to the angels; and if they haven't to be written over again, at least they have to be carried on a few aeons further.

"A CHILD'S HOLIDAY.

"Before the door of a substantial farm-house in the north of Scotland, stands a vehicle of somewhat singular construction. When analysed, however, its composition proves to be simple enough. It is a common agricultural cart, over which, by means of a few iron rods bent across, a semi-cylindrical covering of white canvas has been stretched. It is thus transformed from a hay or harvest cart into a family carriage, of comfortable dimensions, though somewhat slow of progress. The lack of springs is supplied by thick layers of straw, while sacks stuffed with the same material are placed around for seats. Various articles are being stowed away under the bags, and in the corners among the straw, by children with bright expectant faces; the said articles having been in process of collection and arrangement for a month or six weeks previous, in anticipation of the journey which now lies, in all its length and brightness, the length and brightness of a long northern summer's day, before them.

"At last, all their private mysteries of provisions, playthings, and books, having found places of safety more or less accessible on demand, every motion of the horse, every shake and rattle of the covered cart, makes them only more impatient to proceed; which desire is at length gratified by their moving on at a funeral pace through the open gate. They are followed by another cart loaded with the luggage necessary for a six-week's sojourn at one of the fishing villages on the coast, about twenty miles distant from their home. Their father and mother are to follow in the gig, at a later hour in the day, expecting to overtake them about half-way on the road.--Through the neighbouring village they pass, out upon the lonely highway.

"Some seeds are borne to the place of their destiny by their own wings and the wings of the wind, some by the wings of birds, some by simple gravitation. The seed of my story, namely, the covered cart, sent forth to find the soil for its coming growth, is dragged by a stout horse to the sea-shore; and as it oscillates from side to side like a balloon trying to walk, I shall say something of its internal constitution, and principally of its germ; for, regarded as the seed of my story, a pale boy of thirteen is the germ of the cart. First, though he will be of little use to us afterwards, comes a great strong boy of sixteen, who considerably despises this mode of locomotion, believing himself quite capable of driving his mother in the gig, whereas he is only destined to occupy her place in the evening, and return with his father. Then comes the said germ, a boy whom repeated attacks of illness have blanched, and who looks as if the thinness of its earthly garment made his soul tremble with the proximity of the ungenial world. Then follows a pretty blonde, with smooth hair, and smooth cheeks, and bright blue eyes, the embodiment of home pleasures and love; whose chief enjoyment, and earthly destiny indeed, so far as yet revealed, consist in administering to the cupidities of her younger brother, a very ogre of gingerbread men, and Silenus of bottled milk. This milk, by the way, is expected, from former experience, to afford considerable pleasure at the close of the journey, in the shape of one or two pellets of butter in each bottle; the novelty of the phenomenon, and not any scarcity of the article, constituting the ground of interest. A baby on the lap of a rosy country-girl, and the servant in his blue Sunday coat, who sits outside the cover on the edge of the cart, but looks in occasionally to show some attention to the young woman, complete the contents of the vehicle.

"Herbert Netherby, though, as I have said, only thirteen years of age, had already attained a degree of mental development sufficient for characterization. Disease had favoured the almost unhealthy predominance of the mental over the bodily powers of the child; so that, although the constitution which at one time was supposed to have entirely given way, had for the last few years been gradually gaining strength, he was still to be seen far oftener walking about with his hands in his pockets, and his gaze bent on the ground, or turned up to the clouds, than joining in any of the boyish sports of those of his own age. A nervous dread of ridicule would deter him from taking his part, even when for a moment the fountain of youthfulness gushed forth, and impelled him to find rest in activity. So the impulse would pass away, and he would relapse into his former quiescence. But this partial isolation ministered to the growth of a love of Nature which, although its roots were coeval with his being, might not have so soon appeared above ground, but for this lack of human companionship. Thus the boy became one of Nature's favourites, and enjoyed more than a common share of her teaching.

"But he loved her most in her stranger moods. The gathering of a blue cloud, on a sultry summer afternoon, he watched with intense hope, in expectation of a thunder-storm; and a windy night, after harvest, when the trees moaned and tossed their arms about, and the wind ran hither and hither over the desolate fields of stubble, made the child's heart dance within him, and sent him out careering through the deepening darkness. To meet him then, you would not have known him for the sedate, actionless boy, whom you had seen in the morning looking listlessly on while his schoolfellows played. But of all his loves for the shows of Nature, none was so strong as his love for water--common to childhood, with its mills of rushes, its dams, its bridges, its aqueducts; only in Herbert, it was more a quiet, delighted contemplation. Weakness prevented his joining his companions in the river; but the sight of their motions in the mystery of the water, as they floated half-idealized in the clear depth, or glided along by graceful propulsion, gave him as much real enjoyment as they received themselves. For it was water itself that delighted him, whether in rest or motion; whether rippling over many stones, like the first half-articulate sounds of a child's speech, mingled with a strange musical tremble and cadence which the heart only, and not the ear, could detect; or lying in deep still pools, from the bottom of which gleamed up bright green stones, or yet brighter water-plants, cool in their little grotto, with water for an atmosphere and a firmament, through which the sun-rays came, washed of their burning heat, but undimmed of their splendour. He would lie for an hour by the side of a hill-streamlet; he would stand gazing into a muddy pool, left on the road by last night's rain. Once, in such a brown-yellow pool, he beheld a glory--the sun, encircled with a halo vast and wide, varied like the ring of opal colours seen about the moon when she floats through white clouds, only larger and brighter than that. Looking up, he could see nothing but a chaos of black clouds, brilliant towards the sun: the colours he could not see, except in the muddy water.

"In autumn the rains would come down for days, and the river grow stormy, forget its clearness, and spread out like a lake over the meadows; and that was delightful indeed. But greater yet was the delight when the foot-bridge was carried away; for then they had to cross the stream in a boat. He longed for water where it could not be; would fain have seen it running through the grass in front of his father's house; and had a waking vision of a stream with wooden shores that babbled through his bedroom. So it may be fancied with what delight he overheard the parental decision that they should spend some weeks by the shores of the great world--water, the father and the grave of rivers.

"After many vain outlooks, and fruitless inquiries of their driver, a sudden turn in the road brought them in sight of the sea between the hills; itself resembling a low blue hill, covered with white stones. Indeed, the little girl only doubted whether those were white stones or sheep scattered all over it. They lost sight of it; saw it again; and hailed it with greater rapture than at first.

"The sun was more than halfway down when they arrived. They had secured a little cottage, almost on the brow of the high shore, which in most places went down perpendicularly to the beach or sands, and in some right into deep water; but opposite the cottage, declined with a sloping, grassy descent. A winding track led down to the village, which nestled in a hollow, with steep footpaths radiating from it. In front of it, lower still, lay the narrow beach, narrow even at low water, for the steep, rocky shore went steep and rocky down into the abyss. A thousand fantastic rocks stood between land and water; amidst which, at half-tide, were many little rocky arbours, with floors of sunny sand, and three or four feet of water. Here you might bathe, or sit on the ledges with your feet in the water, medicated with the restless glitter and bewilderment of a half-dissolved sunbeam.

"A promontory, curving out into the sea, on the right, formed a bay and natural harbour, from which, towards the setting sun, many fishing-boats were diverging into the wide sea, as the children, stiff and weary, were getting out of the cart. Herbert's fatigue was soon forgotten in watching their brown-dyed sails, glowing almost red in the sunset, as they went out far into the dark, hunters of the deep, to spend the night on the waters.

"From the windows, the children could not see the shore, with all its burst of beauties struck out from the meeting of things unlike; for it lay far down, and the brow of the hill rose between it and them; only they knew that below the waves were breaking on the rocks, and they heard the gush and roar filling all the air. The room in which Herbert slept was a little attic, with a window towards the sea. After gazing with unutterable delight on the boundless water, which lay like a condensed sky in the grey light of the sleeping day (for there is no night at this season in the North), till he saw it even when his eyelids closed from weariness, he lay down, and the monotonous lullaby of the sea mingled with his dreams.

"Next morning he was wakened by the challenging and replying of the sentinel-cocks, whose crowing sounded to him more clear and musical than that of any of the cocks at home. He jumped out of bed. It was a sunny morning, and his soul felt like a flake of sunshine, as he looked out of his window on the radiant sea, green and flashing, its clear surface here and there torn by the wind into spots of opaque white. So happy did he feel, that he might have been one who had slept through death and the judgment, and had awaked, a child, still in the kingdom of God, under the new heavens and upon the new earth.

"After breakfast, they all went down with their mother to the sea-shore. As they went, the last of the boats which had gone out the night before, were returning laden, like bees. The sea had been bountiful. Everything shone with gladness. But as Herbert drew nearer, he felt a kind of dread at the recklessness of the waves. On they hurried, assailed the rocks, devoured the sands, cast themselves in wild abandonment on whatever opposed them. He feared at first to go near, for they were unsympathizing, caring not for his love or his joy, and would sweep him away like one of those floating sea-weeds. 'If they are such in their play,' thought he, 'what must they be in their anger!' But ere long he was playing with the sea as with a tame tiger, chasing the retreating waters till they rallied and he, in his turn, had to flee from their pursuit. Wearied at length, he left his brother and sister building castles of wet sand, and wandered along the shore.

"Everywhere about lay shallow lakes of salt water, so shallow that they were invisible, except when a puff of wind blew a thousand ripples into the sun; whereupon they flashed as if a precipitous rain of stormy light had rushed down upon them. Lifting his eyes from one of these films of water, Herbert saw on the opposite side, stooping to pick up some treasure of the sea, a little girl, apparently about nine years of age. When she raised herself and saw Herbert, she moved slowly away with a quiet grace, that strangely contrasted with her tattered garments. She was ragged like the sea-shore, or the bunch of dripping sea-weed that she carried in her hand; she was bare from foot to knee, and passed over the wet sand with a gleam; the wind had been at more trouble with her hair than any loving hand; it was black, lusterless, and tangled. The sight of rags was always enough to move Herbert's sympathies, and he wished to speak to the little girl, and give her something. But when he had followed her a short distance, all at once, and without having looked round, she began to glide away from him with a wave-like motion, dancing and leaping; till a clear pool in the hollow of a tabular rock imbedded in the sand, arrested her progress. Here she stood like a statue, gazing into its depth; then, with a dart like a kingfisher, plunged half into it, caught something at which her head and curved neck showed that she looked with satisfaction--and again, before Herbert could come near her, was skimming along the uneven shore. He followed, as a boy follows a lapwing; but she, like the lapwing, gradually increased the distance between them, till he gave up the pursuit with some disappointment, and returned to his brother and sister. More ambitious than they, he proceeded to construct--chiefly for the sake of the moat he intended to draw around it--a sand-castle of considerable pretensions; but the advancing tide drove him from his stronghold before he had begun to dig the projected fosse.

"As they returned home, they passed a group of fishermen in their long boots and flapped sou'-westers, looking somewhat anxiously seaward. Much to Herbert's delight, they predicted a stiff gale, and probably a storm. A low bank of cloud had gathered along the horizon, and the wind had already freshened; the white spots were thicker on the waves, and the sound of their trampling on the shore grew louder.

"After dinner, they sat at the window of their little parlour, looking out over the sea, which grew darker and more sullen, ever as the afternoon declined. The cloudy bank had risen and walled out the sun; but a narrow space of blue on the horizon looked like the rent whence the wind rushed forth on the sea, and with the feet of its stormy horses tore up the blue surface, and scattered the ocean-dust in clouds. As evening drew on, Herbert could keep in the house no longer. He wandered away on the heights, keeping from the brow of the cliffs; now and then stooping and struggling with a stormier eddy; till, descending into a little hollow, he sunk below the plane of the tempest, and stood in the glow of a sudden calm, hearing the tumult all round him, but himself in peace. Looking up, he could see nothing but the sides of the hollow with the sky resting on them, till, turning towards the sea, he saw, at some distance, a point of the cliff rising abruptly into the air. At the same moment, the sun looked out from a crack in the clouds, on the very horizon; and as Herbert could not see the sunset, the peculiar radiance illuminated the more strangely the dark vault of earth and cloudy sky. Suddenly, to his astonishment, it was concentrated on the form of the little ragged girl. She stood on the summit of the peak before him. The light was a crown, not to her head only, but to her whole person; as if she herself were the crown set on the brows of the majestic shore. Disappearing as suddenly, it left her standing on the peak, dark and stormy; every tress, if tresses they could be called, of her windy hair, every tatter of her scanty garments, seeming individually to protest, 'The wind is my playmate; let me go!' If Aphrodite was born of the sunny sea, this child was the offspring of the windy shore; as if the mind of the place had developed for itself a consciousness, and this was its embodiment. She bore a strange affinity to the rocks, and the sea-weed, and the pools, and the wide, wild ocean; and Herbert would scarcely have been shocked to see her cast herself from the cliff into the waves, which now dashed half-way up its height. By the time he had got out of the hollow, she had vanished, and where she had gone he could not conjecture. He half feared she had fallen over the precipice; and several times that night, as the vapour of dreams gathered around him, he started from his half-sleep in terror at seeing the little genius of the storm fall from her rock-pedestal into the thundering waves as its foot.

"Next day the wind continuing off the sea, with vapour and rain, the children were compelled to remain within doors, and betake themselves to books and playthings. But Herbert's chief resource lay in watching the sea and the low grey sky, between which was no distinguishable horizon. The wind still increased, and before the afternoon it blew a thorough storm, wind and waves raging together on the rocky shore. The fishermen had secured their boats, drawing them up high on the land; but what vessels might be labouring under the low misty pall no one could tell. Many anxious fears were expressed for some known to be at sea; and many tales of shipwreck were told that night in the storm-shaken cottages.

"The day was closing in, darkened the sooner by the mist, when Herbert, standing at the window, now rather weary, saw the little girl dart past like a petrel. He snatched up his cap and rushed from the house, buttoning his jacket to defend him from the weather. The little fellow, though so quiet among other boys, was a lover of the storm as much as the girl was, and would have preferred its buffeting, so long as his strength lasted, to the warmest nook by the fireside; and now he could not resist the temptation to follow her. As soon as he was clear of the garden, he saw her stopping to gaze down on the sea--starting again along the heights-- blown out of her course--and regaining it by struggling up in the teeth of the storm. He at once hastened in pursuit, trying as much as possible to keep out of her sight, and was gradually lessening the distance between them, when, on crossing the hollow already mentioned, he saw her on the edge of the cliff, close to the pinnacle on which she had stood the night before; where after standing for a moment, she sank downwards and vanished, but whether into earth or air, he could not tell. He approached the place. A blast of more than ordinary violence fought against him, as if determined to preserve the secret of its favourite's refuge. But he persisted, and gained the spot.

"He then found that the real edge of the precipice was several yards farther off, the ground sloping away from where he stood. At his feet, in the slope, was an almost perpendicular opening. He hesitated a little; but, sure that the child was a real human child and no phantom, he did not hesitate long. He entered and found it lead spirally downwards. Descending with some difficulty, for the passage was narrow, he arrived at a small chamber, into one corner of which the stone shaft, containing the stair, projected half its round. The chamber looked as if it had been hollowed out of the rock. A narrow window, little more than a loop-hole through the thick wall, admitted the roar of the waves and a dim grey light. This light was just sufficient to show him the child in the farthest corner of the chamber, bending forward with her hands between her knees, in a posture that indicated fear. The little playfellow of the winds was not sure of him. At the first word he spoke, a sea-bird, which had made its home in the apartment, startled by the sound of his voice, dashed through the window, with a sudden clang of wings, into the great misty void without; and Herbert looking out after it, almost forgot the presence of the little girl in the awe and delight of the spectacle before him. It was now much darker, and the fog had settled down more closely on the face of the deep; but just below him he could see the surface of the ocean, whose mad waves appeared to rush bellowing out of the unseen on to the shore of the visible. When, after some effort, he succeeded in leaning out of the window, he could see the shore beneath him; for he was on its extreme verge, and the spray now and then dashed through the loop-hole into the chamber. He was still gazing and absorbed, when a sweet timid voice, that yet partook undefinably of the wildness of a sea-breeze, startled him out of his contemplation.

"'Did my mother send you to me?' said the voice.

"He looked down. Close beside him stood the child, gazing earnestly up into his face through the twilight from the window.

"'Where does your mother live?' asked Herbert.

"'All out there,' the child answered, pointing to the window.

"While he was thinking what she could mean, she continued:

"'Mother is angry to-night; but when the sun comes out, and those nasty clouds are driven away, she will laugh again. Mother does not like black clouds and fogs; they spoil her house.'

"Still perplexed as to the child's meaning, Herbert asked,

"'Does your mother love you?'

"'Yes, except when she is angry. She does not love me to-night; but to-morrow, perhaps, she will be all over laughs to me; and that makes me run to her; and she will smile to me all day, till night comes and she goes to sleep, and leaves me alone; for I hear her sleeping, but I cannot go to sleep with her.'"

Here the curate interrupted his reading to remark, that he feared he had spoiled the pathos of the child's words, by translating them into English; but that they must gain more, for the occasion, by being made intelligible to his audience, than they could lose by the change from their original form.

"Herbert's sympathies had by this time made him suspect that the child must be talking of the sea, which somehow she had come to regard as her mother. He asked,

"'Where does your father live, then?'

"'I have not any father,' she answered. 'I had one, but mother took him.'

"Several other questions Herbert put; but still the child's notions ran in the same channel. They were wild notions, but uttered with confidence as if they were the most ordinary facts. It seemed that whatever her imagination suggested, bore to her the impress of self-evident truth; and that she knew no higher reality.

"By this time it was almost dark.

"'I must go home,' said Herbert.

"'I will go with you,' responded the girl.

"She ran along beside him, but in the discursive manner natural to her; till, coming to one of the paths descending towards the shore, she darted down, without saying good-night even.

"Next day, the storm having abated, and the sun shining out, they were standing on the beach, near a fisherman, who like them was gazing seawards, when the child went skimming past along the shore. Mrs. Netherby asked the fisherman about her, and learned the secret of the sea's motherhood. She had been washed ashore from the wreck of a vessel; and was found on the beach, tied to a spar. All besides had perished. From the fragment they judged it to have been a Dutch vessel. Some one had said in her hearing--'Poor child! the sea is her mother;' and her imagination had cherished the idea. A fisherman, who had no family, had taken her to his house and loved her dearly. But he lost his wife shortly after; and a year or two ago, the sea had taken him, the only father she knew. All, however, were kind to her. She was welcome wherever she chose to go and share with the family. But no one knew today where she would be to-morrow, where she would have her next meal, or where she would sleep. She was wild, impulsive, affectionate. The simple people of the village believed her to be of foreign birth and high descent, while reverence for her lonely conditions made them treat her with affection as well as deference; so that the forsaken child, regarded as subject to no law, was as happy in her freedom and confidence as any wild winged thing of the land or sea. The summer loved her; the winter strengthened her. Her first baptism in the salt waters had made her a free creature of the earth and skies; had fortified her, Achilles-like, against all hardship, cold, and nakedness to come; had delivered her from the bonds of habit and custom, and shown in her what earth and air of themselves can do, to make the lowest, most undeveloped life, a divine gift.

"The following morning, the sea was smooth and clear. So was the sky. Looking down from their cottage, the sea appeared to Herbert to slope steeply up to the horizon, so that the shore lay like a deep narrow valley between him and it. Far down, at the low pier, he saw a little boat belonging to a retired ship-captain. The oars were on board; and the owner and some one with him were walking towards the boat. Now the captain had promised to take him with him some day.

"He was half-way down the road a moment after the words of permission had left his mother's lips, and was waiting at the boat when the two men came up. They readily agreed to let him go with them. They were going to row to a village on the opposite side of the bay, and return in the evening. Herbert was speechless with delight. They got in, the boat heaving beneath them, unmoored and pushed off. This suspension between sea and sky was a new sensation to Herbert; for when he looked down, his eye did not repose on the surface, but penetrated far into a clear green abyss, where the power of vision seemed rather to vanish than be arrested. When he looked up, the shore was behind them; and he knew, for the first time, what it was to look at the land as he had looked at the sea; to regard the land, in its turn, as a ***phenomenon***--observing it apart from himself.

"Running along the shore like a little bird, he saw the child of the sea; and, further to the right, the peak on which she had stood in the sunset, and into whose mysterious chamber she had led him. The captain here put a pocket-telescope into his hand; and with this annihilator of space he made new discoveries. He saw a little window in the cliff, doubtless the same from which he had looked out on the dim sea; and then perceived that the front of the cliff, in that part, was no rock, but a wall, regularly and strongly built. It was evidently the remains of an old fortress. The front foundation had been laid in the rocks of the shore; the cliff had then been faced up with masonry; and behind chambers had been cut in the rock; into one of which Herbert had descended a ruined spiral stair. The castle itself, which had stood on the top, had mouldered away, leaving only a rugged and broken surface.

"By this time they were near the opposite shore, and Herbert looked up with dread at the great cliffs that rose perpendicularly out of the water, which heaved slowly and heavily, with an appearance of immense depth, against them. Their black jagged sides had huge holes, into which the sea rushed--far into the dark--

with a muffled roar; and large protuberances of rock, bare and threatening. Numberless shadows lay on their faces; and here and there from their tops trickled little steams, plashing into the waves at their feet. Passing through a natural arch in a rock, lofty and narrow, called the Devil's Bridge, and turning a little promontory, they were soon aground on the beach.

"When the captain had finished his business, they had some dinner at the inn; and while the two men drank their grog, Herbert was a delighted listener to many a sea story, old and new. How the boy longed to be a sailor, and live always on the great waters! The blocks and cordage of the fast-rooted flagstaff before the inn, assumed an almost magic interest to him, as the two sailors went on with their tales of winds and rocks, and narrow escapes and shipwrecks. And how proud he was of the friendship of these old seafarers!

"At length it was time to return home. As they rowed slowly along, the sun was going down in the west, and their shadows were flung far on the waves, which gleamed and glistened in the rich calm light. Land and sea were bathed in the blessing of heaven; its glory was on the rocks, and on the shore, and in the depth of the heaving sea. Under the boat, wherever it went, shone a paler green. The only sounds were of the oars in the row-locks, of the drip from their blades as they rose and made curves in the air, and the low plash with which they dipped again into the sea; while the water in the wake of the boat hastened to compose itself again to that sleep from which it had been unwillingly roused by the passing keel. The boy's heart was full. Often in after years he longed for the wings of a dove that he might fly to that boat (still floating in the calm sea of his memory), and there lie until his spirit had had rest enough.

"The next time that Herbert approached the little girl, she waited his coming; and while they talked, Mrs. Netherby joined them with her Effie. Presently the gaze of the sea-child was fixed upon little Effie, to the all but total neglect of the others. The result of this contemplation was visible the next day. Mrs. Netherby having invited her to come and see them, the following morning, as they were seated at breakfast, the door of the room opened, without any prefatory tap, and in peeped with wild confidence the smiling face of the untamed Undine. It was at once evident that civilization had laid a finger upon her, and that a new womanly impulse had been awakened. For there she stood, gazing at Effie, and with both hands smoothing down her own hair, which she had managed, after a fashion, to part in the middle, and had plentifully wetted with sea-water. In her run up the height, it had begun to dry, and little spangles of salt were visible all over it. She could not alter her dress, whose many slashes showed little lining except her skin; but she had done all she could to approximate her appearance to that of Effie, whom she seemed to regard as a little divinity.

"Mrs. Netherby's heart was drawn towards the motherless child, and she clothed her from head to foot; though how far this was a benefit as regarded cold and heat, is a question. Herbert began to teach her to read; in which her progress was just like her bodily movements over the earth's surface; now a dead pause, and now the flight of a bird. Now and then she would suddenly start up, heedless where her book might happen to fall, and rush out along the heights; returning next day, or the same afternoon, and, without any apology, resuming her studies.

"This holiday was to Herbert one of those seasons which tinge the whole of the future life. It was a storehouse of sights and sounds and images of thought; a tiring-room, wherein to clothe the ideas that came forth to act their parts upon the stage of reason. Often at night, just ere the sleep that wipes out the day from the overfilled and blotted tablets of the brain, enwrapped him in its cool, grave-like garments, a vision of the darkened sea, spotted and spangled with pools of unutterable light, would rise before him unbidden, in that infinite space for creation which lies dark and waiting under the closed eyelids. The darkened sea might be but the out-thrown image of his own overshadowed soul; and the spots of light the visual form of his hopes. So clearly would these be present to him sometimes, that when he opened his eyes and gazed into the darkness of his room, he would see the bright spaces shining before him still. Then he would fall asleep and dream on about the sea--watching a little cutter perhaps, as 'she leaned to the lee, and girdled the wave,' flinging the frolic-some waters from her bows, and parting a path for herself between. Or he would be seated with the helm in his hand, and all the force and the joy wherewith she dashed headlong on the rising waves, and half pierced them and half drove them under her triumphant keel, would be issuing from his will and his triumph.

"Surely even for the sad despairing waves there is some hope, out in that boundless room which borders on the sky, and upon which, even in the gloomiest hour of tempest, falls sometimes from heaven a glory intense.

"So when the time came that the lover of waters must return, he went back enriched with new visions of them in their great home and motherland, he had seen them still and silent as a soul in holy trance; he had seen them raving in a fury of livid green, swarming with 'white-mouthed waves;' he had seen them lying in one narrow ridge of unbroken blue, where the eye, finding no marks to measure the distance withal, saw miles as furlongs; and he had seen sweeps and shadows innumerable stretched along its calm expanse, so dividing it into regions, and graduating the distance, that the eye seemed to wander on and on from sea to sea, and the ships to float in oceans beyond oceans of infinite reach. O lonely space! awful indeed wert thou, did no one love us! But he had yet to receive one more vision of the waters, and that was to be in a dream. With this dream I will close the story of his holiday; for it went with him ever after, breaking forth from the dream-home, and encompassing his waking thoughts with an atmosphere of courage and hope, when his heart was ready to sink in a world which was not the world the boy had thought to enter, when he ran to welcome his fate.

"On their last Sunday, Herbert went with his mother to the evening service in a little chapel in the midst of the fishermen's cottages. It was a curious little place, with galleries round, that nearly met in the middle, and a high pulpit with a great sounding-board over it, from which came the voice of an earnest little Methodist, magnified by his position into a mighty prophet. The good man was preaching on the parable of ***the sheep and the goats;*** and, in his earnestness for his own theology and the souls of his hearers, was not content that the Lord should say these things in his own way, but he must say them in his too. And a terrible utterance it was! Looking about, unconsciously seeking some relief from the accumulation of horrors with which the preacher was threatening the goats of his congregation, Herbert spied, in the very front of one of the side galleries, his little pupil, white with terror, and staring with round unwinking eyes full in the face of the prophet of fear. Never after could he read the parable without seeing the blanched face of the child, and feeling a renewal of that evening's sadness over the fate of the poor goats which afterwards grew into the question--'Doth God care for oxen, and not for goats?' He never saw the child again; for they left the next day, and she did not come to bid them good-by.

"As he went home from the chapel, her face of terror haunted him.

"That night he fell asleep, as usual, with the sound of the waves in his soul. And as he slept he dreamed.--He stood, as he thought, upon the cliff, within which lay the remnants of the old castle. The sun was slowly sinking down the western sky, and a great glory lay upon the sea. Close to the shore beneath, by the side of some low rocks, floated a little boat. He thought how delightful it would be to lie in the boat in the sunlight, and let it die away upon his bosom. He scrambled down the rocks, stepped on board, and laid himself in the boat, with his face turned towards the sinking sun. Lower and lower the sun sank, seeming to draw the heavens after him, like a net. At length he plunged beneath the waves; but as his last rays disappeared on the horizon, lo! a new splendour burst upon the astonished boy. The whole waters were illuminated from beneath, with the permeating glories of the buried radiance. In rainbow circles, and intermingling, fluctuating sweeps of colours, the sea lay like an intense opal, molten with the fire of its own hues. The sky gave back the effulgence with a less deep but more heavenly loveliness.

"But betwixt the sea and the sky, just over the grave of the down-gone sun, a dark spot appeared, parting the earth and the heaven where they had mingled in embraces of light. And the dark spot grew and spread, and a cold breath came softly over the face of the shining waters; and the colours paled away; and as the blossom-sea withered and grew grey below, the clouds withered and darkened above. The sea began to swell and moan and look up, like the soul of a man whose joy is going down in darkness; and a horror came over the heart of the sleeper, and in his dream he lifted up his head, meaning to rise and hasten to his home. But, behold, the shore was far away, and the great castle-cliff had sunk to a low ridge! With a cry, he sank back on the bosom of the careless sea.

"The boat began to rise and fall on the waking waves. Then a great blast of wind laid hold of it, and whirled it about. Once more he looked up, and saw that the tops of the waves were torn away, and that 'the white water was coming out of the black.' Higher and higher rose the billows; louder and louder roared the wind across their jagged furrows, tearing awful descants from their bursting chords, and tossing the little boat like a leaf in the lone desert of storms; now holding it perched on the very crest of a wave, in the mad eye of the tempest, while the chaotic waters danced, raving about, in hopeless confusion; now letting it sink in the hollow of the waves, and lifting above it cold glittering walls of water, that becalmed it as in a sheltered vale, while the hurricane roaring above, flung arches of writhing waters across from billow to billow overhead, and threatened to close, as in a transparent tomb, boat and boy. At length, when the boat rose once more, unwilling, to the awful ridge, jagged and white, a yet fiercer blast tore it from the top of the wave. The dreamer found himself choking in the waters, and soon lost all consciousness of the buffeting waves or the shrieking winds.

"When the dreamer again awoke, he felt that he was carried along through the storm above the waves; for they reached him only in bursts of spray, though the wind raged around him more fiercely than ever. He opened his eyes and looked downwards. Beneath him seethed and boiled the tumultuous billows, their wreathy tops torn from them, and shot, in long vanishing sheets of spray, over the distracted wilderness. Such was the turmoil beneath, that he had to close his eyes again to feel that he was moving onwards.

"The next time he opened them, it was to look up. And lo! a shadowy face bent over him, whence love unutterable was falling in floods, from eyes deep, and dark, and still, as the heavens that are above the clouds, Great waves of hair streamed back from a noble head, and floated on the tides of the tempest. The face was like his mother's and like his father's, and like a face that he had seen somewhere in a picture, but far more beautiful and strong and loving than all. With a sudden glory of gladness, in which the spouting pinnacles of the fathomless pyramids of wandering waters dwindled into the confusion of a few troubled water-drops, he knew, he knew that the Lord was carrying his lamb in his bosom. Around him were the everlasting arms, and above him the lamps that light heaven and earth, the eyes that watch and are not weary. And now he felt the arms in which he lay, and he nestled close to that true, wise bosom, which has room in it for all, and where none will strive.

"Over the waters went the Master, now crossing the calm hollows, now climbing the rising wave, now shrouded in the upper ocean of drifting spray, that wrapped him around with whirling force, and anon calmly descending the gliding slope into the glassy trough below. Sometimes, when he looked up, the dreamer could see nothing but the clouds driving across the heavens, whence now and then a star, in a little well of blue, looked down upon him; but anon he knew that the driving clouds were his drifting hair, and that the stars in the blue wells of heaven were his love-lighted eyes. Over the sea he strode, and the floods lifted up their heads in vain. The billows would gather and burst around and over them; but a moment more, and the billows were beneath his feet, and on they were going, safe and sure.

"Long time the journey endured; and the dream faded and again revived. It was as if he had slept, and again awaked; for he lay in soft grass on a mountain-side, and the form of a mighty man lay outstretched beside him, who was weary with a great weariness.

"Below, the sea howled and beat against the base of the mountain; but it was far below. Again the Lord arose, and lifted him up, and bore him onwards. Up to the mountain-top they went, through the keen, cold air, and over the fields of snow and ice. On the peak the Master paused and looked down.

"In a vast amphitheatre below, was gathered a multitude that no man could number. They crowded on all sides beyond the reach of the sight, rising up the slopes of the surrounding mountains, till they could no longer be distinguished; grouped and massed upon height above height; filling the hollows, and plains, and platforms all about. But every eye looked towards the lowest centre of the mountain-amphitheatre, where a little vacant spot awaited the presence of some form, which should be the heart of all the throng. Down towards this centre the Lord bore him. Entering the holy circle, he set him gently down, and then looked all around, as if searching earnestly for some one he could not see.

"And not finding whom he sought, he walked across the open space. A path was instantly divided for him through the dense multitude surrounding it. Along this lane of men and women and children, he went; and Herbert ran, following close at his feet; for now all the universe seemed empty save where he was. And he was not rebuked, but suffered to follow. And although the Lord walked fast and far, the feet following him were not weary, but grew in speed and in power. Through the great crowd and beyond it, never looking back, up and over the brow of the mountain they went, and leaving behind them the gathered universe of men, descended into a pale night. Hither and hither went the Master, searching up and down the gloomy valley; now looking behind a great rock, and now through a thicket of brushwood; now entering a dark cave, and now ascending a height and gazing all around; till at last, on a bare plain, seated on a grey stone, with her hands in her lap, they found the little orphan child who had called the sea her mother.

"As he drew near to her, the Lord called out, 'My poor little lamb, I have found you at last!' But she did not seem to hear or understand what he said; for she fell on her knees, and held up her clasped hands, and cried, 'Do not be angry with me. I am a goat; and I ran away because I was afraid. Do not burn me.' But all the answer the Lord made was to stoop, and lift her, and hold her to his breast. And she was an orphan no more.

"So he turned and went back over hill and over dale, and Herbert followed, rejoicing that the lost lamb was found.

"As he followed, he spied in a crevice of a rock, close by his path, a lovely primrose. He stooped to pluck it. And ere he began again to follow, a cock crew shrill and loud; and he knew it was the cock that rebuked Peter; and he trembled and stood up. The Master had vanished. He, too, fell a-weeping bitterly. And again the cock crew; and he opened his eyes, and knew that he had dreamed. His mother stood by his bedside, comforting the weeper with kisses. And he cried to her--

"'O mother! surely he would not come over the sea to find me in the storm, and then leave me because I stopped to pluck a flower!'"

* * * * *

"Too long, I am afraid," said the curate, the moment he had finished his paper, looking at his watch.

"We have not thought so, I am sure," said Adela, courteously. The ladies rose to go.

"Who is to read next?" said the schoolmaster.

"Why, of course," said the curate, indignantly, "it ought to be my brother, but there is no depending on him."

"If this frost lasts, I will positively read next time," said the doctor. "But, you know, Ralph, it will be better for you to bring something else with you, lest I should fail again."

"Cool!" said the curate. "I think it is time we dropped it."

"No, please don't," said Harry, with a little anxiety in his tone. "I really want to read my story."

"It looks like it, doesn't it?"

"Now, Ralph, a clergyman should never be sarcastic. Be as indignant as you please--but--sarcastic--never. It is very easy for you, who know just what you have to do, and have besides whole volumes in that rickety old desk of yours, to keep such an appointment as this. Mine is produced for the occasion, ***bona fide***; and I cannot tell what may be required of me from one hour to another."

He went up to Adela.

"I am very sorry to have failed again," he said.

"But you won't next time, will you?"

"I will not, if I can help it."

CHAPTER IV.
INTERRUPTION.

But it was Adela herself who failed next time. I had seen her during the reading draw her shawl about her as if she were cold. She seemed quite well when the friends left, but she had caught a chill; and before the morning she was quite feverish, and unable to leave her bed.

"You see, Colonel," said Mrs. Cathcart at breakfast, "that this doctor of yours is doing the child harm instead of good. He has been suppressing instead of curing the complaint; and now she is worse than ever."

"When the devil--" I began to remark in reply.

"Mr. Smith!" exclaimed Mrs. Cathcart.

"Allow me, madam, to finish my sentence before you make up your mind to be shocked.--When the devil goes out of a man, or a woman either, he gives a terrible wrench by way of farewell. Now, as the prophet Job teaches us, all disease is from the devil; and--"

"The prophet Job!--Mr. Smith?"

"Well, the old Arab Scheik, if you like that epithet better."

"Really, Mr. Smith!"

"Well, I don't mind what you call him. I only mean to say that a disease sometimes goes out with a kind of flare, like a candle--or like the poor life itself. I believe, if this is an intermittent fever--as, from your description, I expect it will prove to be--it will be the best thing for her."

"Well, we shall see what Dr. Wade will say."

"Dr. Wade?" I exclaimed.

"Of course, my brother will not think of trusting such a serious case to an inexperienced young man like Mr. Armstrong."

"It seems to me," I replied, "that for some time the case has ceased to be a serious one. You must allow that Adela is better."

"Seemed to be better, Mr. Smith. But it was all excitement, and here is the consequence. I, as far as I have any influence, decidedly object to Mr. Armstrong having anything more to do with the case."

"Perhaps you are right, Jane," said the colonel. "I fear you are. But how can I ask Dr. Wade to resume his attendance?"

Always nervous about Adela, his sister-in-law had at length succeeded in frightening him.

"Leave that to me," she said; "I will manage him."

"Pooh!" said I, rudely. "He will jump at it. It will be a grand triumph for him. I only want you to mind what you are about. You know Adela does not like Dr. Wade."

"And she does like ***Doctor*** Armstrong?" said Mrs. Cathcart, stuffing each word with significance.

"Yes," I answered, boldly. "Who would not prefer the one to the other?"

But her arrow had struck. The colonel rose, and saying only, "Well, Jane, I leave the affair in your hands," walked out of the room. I was coward enough to follow him. Had it been of any use, coward as I was, I would have remained.

But Mrs. Cathcart, if she had not reckoned without her host, had, at least, reckoned without her hostess. She wrote instantly to Dr. Wade, in terms of which it is enough to say that they were successful, for they brought the doctor at once. I saw him pass through the hall, looking awfully stiff, important, and condescending. Beeves, who had opened the door to him, gave me a very queer look as he showed him into the drawing-room, ringing, at the same time, for Adela's maid.

Now Mrs. Cathcart had not expected that the doctor would arrive so soon, and had, as yet, been unable to make up her mind how to communicate to the patient the news of the change in the physical ministry. So when the maid brought the message, all that her cunning could provide her with at the moment was the pretence, that he had called so opportunely by chance.

"Ask him to walk up," she said, after just one moment's hesitation.

Adela heard the direction her aunt gave, through the cold shiver which was then obliterating rather than engrossing her attention, and concluded that they had sent for Mr. Armstrong. But Mrs. Cathcart, turning towards her, said--

"Adela, my love, Dr. Wade had just called; and I have asked him to step up stairs."

The patient started up.

"Aunt, what do you mean? If that old wife comes into this room, I will make him glad to go out of it!"

You see she was feverish, poor child, else I am sure she could not have been so rude to her aunt. But before Mrs. Cathcart could reply, in came Dr. Wade. He walked right up to the bed, after a stately obeisance to the lady attendant.

"I am sorry to find you so ill, Miss Cathcart."

"I am perfectly well, Dr. Wade. I am sorry you have had the trouble of walking up stairs."

As she said this, she rang the bell at the head of her bed. Her maid, who had been listening at the door, entered at once.--I had all this from Adela herself afterwards.

"Emma, bring me my desk. Dr. Wade, there must be some mistake. It was my aunt, Mrs. Cathcart, who sent for you. Had she given me the opportunity, I would have begged that the interview might take place in her room instead of mine."

Dr. Wade retreated towards the fireplace, where Mrs. Cathcart stood, quite aware that she had got herself into a mess of no ordinary complication. Yet she persisted in her cunning. She lifted her finger to her forehead.

"Ah?" said Dr. Wade.

"Yes," said Mrs. Cathcart.

"Wandering?"

"Dreadfully."

After some more whispering, the doctor sat down to write a prescription. But meantime, Adela was busy writing another. What she wrote was precisely to this effect--

"Dear Mr. Armstrong,

"I have caught a bad cold, and my aunt has let loose Dr. Wade upon me. Please come directly, if you will save me from ever so much nasty medicine, at the least. My aunt is not my mother, thank heaven! though she would gladly usurp that relationship.

"Yours most truly,

"Adela Cathcart."

She folded and sealed the note--sealed it carefully--and gave it to Emma, who vanished with it, followed instantly by Mrs. Cathcart. As to what took place outside the door--shall I confess it?--Beeves is my informant.

"Where are you going, Emma? Emma, come here directly," said Mrs. Cathcart.

Emma obeyed.

"I am going a message for mis'ess."

"Who is that note for?"

"I didn't ask. John can read well enough."

"Show it me."

Emma, I presume, closed both lips and hand very tight. "I command you."

"Miss Cathcart pays me my wages, ma'am," said Emma, and turning, sped down-stairs like a carrier-pigeon.

In the hall she met Beeves, and told him the story.

"There she comes!" cried he. "Give me the letter. I'll take it myself."

"You're not going without your hat, surely, Mr. Beeves," said Emma.

"Bless me! It's down-stairs. There's master's old one! He'll never want it again. And if he does, it'll be none the worse."

And he was out of the door in a moment. Beeves's alarm, however, as to Mrs. Cathcart's approach, was a false one. She returned into the sick chamber, with a face fiery red, and found Dr. Wade just finishing an elaborate prescription.

"There!" said he, rising. "Send for that at once, and let it be taken directly. Good morning."

He left the room instantly, making signs that he was afraid of exciting his patient, as she did not appear to approve of his presence.

"What is the prescription?" said Adela, quite quietly, as Mrs. Cathcart approached the bed, apparently trying to decipher it.

"I am glad to see you so much calmer, my dear. You must not excite yourself. The prescription?--I cannot make it out. Doctors do write so badly. I suppose they consider it professional."

"They consider a good many things professional which are only stupid. Let me see it."

Mrs. Cathcart, thrown off her guard, gave it to her. Adela tore it in fragments, and threw it in a little storm on the floor.

"Adela!" screamed Mrs. Cathcart. "What is to be done?"

"Pay Dr. Wade his fee, and tell him I shall never be too ill to refuse his medicines. Now, aunt! You find I am determined.--I declare you make me behave so ill that I am ashamed of myself."

Here the poor impertinent child crept under the clothes, and fell a-weeping bitterly. Mrs. Cathcart had sense enough to see that nothing could be done, and retired to her room. Getting weary of her own society after a few moments of solitude, she proceeded to go down-stairs. But half-way down, she was met full in the face by Harry Armstrong ascending two steps at a time. He had already met Dr. Wade, as he came out of the dining-room, where he had been having an interview with the colonel. Harry had turned, and held out his hand with a "How do you do, Dr. Wade?" But that gentleman had bowed with the utmost stiffness, and kept his hand at home.

"So it is to be open war and mutual slander, is it, Dr. Wade?" said Harry. "In that case, I want to know how you come to interfere with my patient. I have had no dismissal, which punctilio I took care to know was observed in your case."

"Sir, I was sent for," said Dr. Wade, haughtily.

"I have in my pocket a note from the lady of this house, requesting my immediate attendance. If you have received a request to the same purport from a visitor, you obey it at your own risk. Good morning."

Then Harry walked quietly up the first half of the stair, while Beeves hastened to open the door to the crest-fallen Dr. Wade; but by the time he met Mrs. Cathcart, his rate of ascent had considerably increased. As soon as she saw him, however, without paying any attention to the usual formality of a greeting, she turned and re-entered her niece's room. Her eyes were flashing, and her face spotted red and white with helpless rage. But she would not abandon the field. Harry bowed to her, and passed on to the bed, where he was greeted with a smile.

"There's not much the matter, I hope?" he said, returning the smile.

"It may suit you to make light of my niece's illness, Mr. Armstrong; but I beg to inform you that her father thought it serious enough to send for Dr. Wade. He has been here already, and your attendance is quite superfluous."

"No doubt; no doubt. But as I am here, I may as well prescribe."

"Dr. Wade has already prescribed."

"And I have taken his prescription, have I not, aunt?--and destroyed it, Mr. Armstrong, instead of my own chance."

"Of what?" said Mrs. Cathcart, with vulgar significance.

"Of getting rid of two officious old women at once," said Adela--in a rage, I fear I must confess, as the only excuse for impertinence.

"Come, come," said Harry, "this won't do. I cannot have my patient excited in this way. Miss Cathcart, may I ring for your maid?"

For answer, Adela rang the bell herself. Her aunt was pretending to look out of the window.

"Will you go and ask your master," said Harry, when Emma made her appearance, "to be so kind as come here for a moment?"

The poor colonel--an excellent soldier, a severe master, with the highest notions of authority and obedience, found himself degraded by his own conduct, as other autocrats have proved before, into a temporizing incapable. It was the more humiliating that he was quite aware in his own honest heart that it was jealousy of Harry that had brought him into this painful position. But he obeyed the summons at once; for wherever there was anything unpleasant to be done, there, with him, duty assumed the sterner command. As soon as he entered the room, Harry, without giving time for anyone else to determine the course of the conference, said:

"There has been some mistake, Colonel Cathcart, between Dr. Wade and myself, which has already done Miss Cathcart no good. As I find her very feverish, though not by any means alarmingly ill, I must, as her medical attendant, insist that ***no*** one come into her room but yourself or her maid."

Every one present perfectly understood this; and however, in other circumstances, the colonel might have resented the tone of authority with which Harry spoke, he was compelled, for his daughter's sake, to yield; and he afterwards justified Harry entirely. Mrs. Cathcart walked out of the room with her neck invisible from behind. The colonel sat down by the fire. Harry wrote his prescription on the half sheet from which Dr. Wade had torn his; and then saying that he would call in the evening, took his leave of the colonel, and bowed to his patient, receiving a glance of acknowledgment which could not fail to generate the feeling that there was a secret understanding between them, and that he had done just what she wanted. He mounted his roan horse, called Rhubarb, with a certain elation of being, which he tried to hide from everyone but himself.

When doctors forget that their patients are more like musical instruments than machines, they will soon need to be reminded that they are men and women, and not dogs or horses. Yet, alas for the poor dogs and horses that fall into the hands of a man without a human sympathy even with them! I, John Smith, bless you, my doctor-friends, that ye are not doctors merely, but good and loving men; and, in virtue thereof, so much the more--so exceedingly the more ***Therapeutae***.

I need not follow the course of the fever. Each day the arrival of the cold fit was longer delayed, and the violence of both diminished, until they disappeared altogether. But a day or two before this happy result was completed, Adela had been allowed to go down to the drawing-room, and had delighted her father with her cheerfulness and hopefulness. It really seemed as if the ague had carried off the last remnants of the illness under which she had been so long labouring. But then, you can never put anything to the ***experimentum crucis***; and there were other causes at work for Adela's cure, which were perhaps more powerful than even the ague. However this may have been, she got almost quite well in a very short space of time; and with her father's consent, issued invitations to another meeting of the story-club. They were at once satisfactorily responded to.

CHAPTER V.
PERCY.

By this time Percy had returned to London. His mother remained; but the terms understood between her niece and herself were those of icy politeness and reserve. I learned afterwards that something of an understanding had also been arrived at between Percy and Harry; ever since learning the particulars of which, I have liked the young rascal a great deal better. So I will trouble my reader to take an interest in my report of the affair.

Percy met Harry at the gate, after one of his professional visits, and accosted him thus:

"Mr. Armstrong, my mother says you have been rude to her."

"I am not in the least aware of it, Mr. Percy."

"Oh! I don't care much. She is provoking. Besides, she can take care of herself. That's not it."

"What is it, then?"

"What do you mean about Adela?"

"I have said nothing more than that she has had a sharp attack of intermittent fever, which is going off."

"Come, come--you know what I mean."

"I may suspect, but I don't choose to answer hints, the meaning of which I ***only*** suspect. I might make a fool of myself."

"Well, I'll be plain. Are you in love with her?"

"Suppose I were, you are not the first to whom I should think it necessary to confess."

"Well, are you paying your addresses to her?"

"I am sorry I cannot consent to make my answers as frank as your questions.

You have the advantage of me in straightforwardness, I confess. Only you have got sun and wind of me both."

"Come, come--I hate dodging."

"I daresay you do. But just let me shift round a bit, and see what you will do then.--Are ***you in love with Miss Cathcart?"***

"Yes."

"Upon my word, I shouldn't have thought it. Here have we been all positively conspiring to do her good, and you have been paying ten times the attention to the dogs and horses that you have paid to her."

"By Jove! it's quite true. But I couldn't somehow."

"Then she hasn't encouraged you?"

"By Jupiter! you are frank enough now.--No, damn it--not a bit.--But she used to like me, and she would again, if you would let her alone."

"Now, Mr. Percy, I'll tell you what.--I don't believe you are a bit in love with her."

"She's devilish pretty."

"Well?"

"And I declare I think she got prettier and prettier every day till this cursed ague took her.--Your fault too, my mother says."

"We'll leave your mother out of the question now, if you please. Do you know what made her look prettier and prettier--for you are quite right about that?"

"No. I suppose you were giving her arsenic."

"No. I was giving her the true elixir vitae, unknown even to the Rosicrucians."

Percy stared.

"I will explain myself. Her friend, Mr. Smith--"

"Old fogie!"

"Old bachelor--yes.--Mr. Smith and I agreed that she was dying of ennui; and so we got up this story-club, and got my brother and the rest to bear a hand in it. It did her all the good the most sanguine of us could have hoped for."

"I thought it horrid slow."

"I am surprised at that, for you were generally asleep."

"I was forced, in self-defence. I couldn't smoke."

"It gave her something to think about."

"So it seems."

"Now, Mr. Percy, how could you think you had the smallest chance with her, when here was the first one and then another turning each the flash of his own mental prism upon her weary eyes, and healing them with light; while you would not take the smallest trouble to gratify her, or even to show yourself to anything like advantage?--My dear fellow, what a fool you are!"

"Mr. Armstrong!"

"Come, come--you began with frankness, and I've only gone on with it. You are a good-hearted fellow, and ought to be made something of."

"At all events, you make something of yourself, to talk of your own productions as the elixir ***vitae***."

"You forget that I am in disgrace as well as yourself on that score; for I have not read a word of my own since the club began."

"Then how the devil should I be worse off than you?"

"I didn't say you were. I only said you did your best to place yourself at a disadvantage. I at least took a part in the affair, although a very humble one. But depend upon it, a girl like Miss Cathcart thinks more of mental gifts, than of any outward advantages which a man may possess; and in the company of those who ***think***, a fellow's good looks don't go for much. She could not help measuring you by those other men--and women too. But you may console yourself with the reflection that there are plenty of girls, and pretty ones too, of a very different way of judging; and for my part you are welcome to the pick of them."

"You mean to say that I sha'n't have Addie?"

"Not in the least. But, come now--do you think yourself worthy of a girl like that?"

"No. Do you?"

"No. But I should not feel such a hypocrite if she thought me worthy, as to give her up on that ground."

"Then what ***do*** you mean?"

"To win her, if I can."

"Whew!"

"But if you are a gentleman, you will let me say so myself, and not betray my secret."

"Damned if I do! Good luck to you! There's my hand. I believe you're a good fellow after all. I wish I had seen you ride to hounds. They tell me it's a sight."

"Thank you heartily. But what are you going to do?"

"Go back to the sweet-flowing Thames, and the dreams of the desk."

"Well--be a man as well as a gentleman. Don't be a fool."

"Hang it all! I believe it was her money, after all, I was in love with. Good-bye!"

But the poor fellow looked grave enough as he went away. And I trust that, before long, he, too, began to reap some of the good corn that grows on the wintry fields of disappointment.--I have my eye upon him; but it is little an ***old fogie*** like me can do with a fellow like Percy.

CHAPTER VI
THE CRUEL PAINTER.

Now to return to the Story-Club.

On the night appointed, we met. And to the delight of all the rest of us, Harry arrived with a look that satisfied us that he was to be no defaulter this time. The look was one of almost nervous uneasiness. Of course this sprung from anxiety to please Adela--at least, so I interpreted it. She occupied her old place on the couch; we all arranged ourselves nearly as before; and the fire was burning very bright. Before he began, however, Harry, turning to our host, said:

"May I arrange the scene as I please, for the right effect of my story?"

"Certainly," answered the colonel.

Harry rose, and extinguished the lamp.

"But, my dear sir," said the colonel, "how can you read now?"

"Perfectly, by the firelight," answered Harry.

He then went to the windows, and drawing aside the curtains, drew up the blinds.

It was full high moon, and the light so clear that, notwithstanding the brightness of the fire, each window seemed to lie in ghostly shimmer on the floor. Not a breath of wind was abroad. The whole country being covered with snow, the air was filled with a snowy light. On one side rose the high roof of another part of the house, on which the snow was lying thick and smooth, undisturbed save by the footprints, visible in the moon, of a large black cat, which had now paused in the middle of it, and was looking round suspiciously towards the source of the light which had surprised him in his midnight walk.

"Now," said Harry, returning to his seat, and putting on an air of confidence to conceal the lack of it, "let any one who has nerves retire at once, both for his own sake and that of the company! This is just such a night as I wanted to read my story in--snow--stillness--moonlight outside, and nothing but firelight inside. Mind, Ralph, you keep up the fire, for the room will be more ready to get cold now the coverings are off the windows.--You will say at once if you feel it cold, Miss Cathcart?"

Adela promised; and Harry, who had his manuscript gummed together in a continuous roll, so that he might not have to turn over any leaves, began at once:

"THE CRUEL PAINTER.

"Among the young men assembled at the University of Prague, in the year 159--, was one called Karl von Wolkenlicht. A somewhat careless student, he yet held a fair position in the estimation of both professors and men, because he could hardly look at a proposition without understanding it. Where such proposition, however, had to do with anything relating to the deeper insights of the nature, he was quite content that, for him, it should remain a proposition; which, however, he laid up in one of his mental cabinets, and was ready to reproduce at a moment's notice. This mental agility was more than matched by the corresponding corporeal excellence, and both aided in producing results in which his remarkable strength was equally apparent. In all games depending upon the combination of muscle and skill, he had scarce rivalry enough to keep him in practice. His strength, however, was embodied in such a softness of muscular outline, such a rare Greek-like style of beauty, and associated with such a gentleness of manner and behaviour, that, partly from the truth of the resemblance, partly from the absurdity of the contrast, he was known throughout the university by the diminutive of the feminine form of his name, and was always called Lottchen.

"'I say, Lottchen,' said one of his fellow-students, called Richter, across the table in a wine-cellar they were in the habit of frequenting, 'do you know, Heinrich Hoellenrachen here says that he saw this morning, with mortal eyes, whom do you think?--Lilith.'

"'Adam's first wife?' asked Lottchen, with an attempt at carelessness, while his face flushed like a maiden's.

"'None of your chaff!'said Richter. 'Your face is honester than your tongue, and confesses what you cannot deny, that you would give your chance of salvation--a small one to be sure, but all you've got--for one peep at Lilith. Wouldn't you now,

Lottchen?'

"'Go to the devil!' was all Lottchen's answer to his tormentor; but he turned to Heinrich, to whom the students had given the surname above mentioned, because of the enormous width of his jaws, and said with eagerness and envy, disguising them as well as he could, under the appearance of curiosity:

"'You don't mean it, Heinrich? You've been taking the beggar in! Confess now.'

"'Not I. I saw her with my two eyes.'

"'Notwithstanding the different planes of their orbits,' suggested Richter.

"'Yes, notwithstanding the fact that I can get a parallax to any of the fixed stars in a moment, with only the breadth of my nose for the base,' answered Heinrich, responding at once to the fun, and careless of the personal defect insinuated. 'She was near enough for even me to see her perfectly.'

"'When? Where? How?' asked Lottchen.

"'Two hours ago. In the churchyard of St. Stephen's. By a lucky chance. Any more little questions, my child?' answered Hoellenrachen.

"'What could have taken her there, who is seen nowhere?' said Richter.

"She was seated on a grave. After she left, I went to the place; but it was a new-made grave. There was no stone up. I asked the sexton about her. He said he supposed she was the daughter of the woman buried there last Thursday week. I knew it was Lilith.'

"'Her mother dead!' said Lottchen, musingly. Then he thought with himself--'She will be going there again, then!' But he took care that this ghost-thought should wander unembodied. 'But how did you know her, Heinrich? You never saw her before.'

"'How do you come to be over head and ears in love with her, Lottchen, and you haven't seen her at all?' interposed Richter.

"'Will you or will you not go to the devil?' rejoined Lottchen, with a comic crescendo; to which the other replied with a laugh.

"'No one could miss knowing her,' said Heinrich.

"'Is she so very like, then?'

"'It is always herself, her very self.'

"A fresh flask of wine, turning out to be not up to the mark, brought the current of conversation against itself; not much to the dissatisfaction of Lottchen, who had already resolved to be in the churchyard of St. Stephen's at sun-down the following day, in the hope that he too might be favoured with a vision of Lilith.

"This resolution he carried out. Seated in a porch of the church, not knowing in what direction to look for the apparition he hoped to see, and desirous as well of not seeming to be on the watch for one, he was gazing at the fallen rose-leaves of the sunset, withering away upon the sky; when, glancing aside by an involuntary movement, he saw a woman seated upon a new-made grave, not many yards from where he sat, with her face buried in her hands, and apparently weeping bitterly. Karl was in the shadow of the porch, and could see her perfectly, without much danger of being discovered by her; so he sat and watched her. She raised her head for a moment, and the rose-flush of the west fell over it, shining on the tears with which it was wet, and giving the whole a bloom which did not belong to it, for it was always pale, and now pale as death. It was indeed the face of Lilith, the most celebrated beauty of Prague.

"Again she buried her face in her hands; and Karl sat with a strange feeling of helplessness, which grew as he sat; and the longing to help her whom he could not help, drew his heart towards her with a trembling reverence which was quite new to him. She wept on. The western roses withered slowly away, and the clouds blended with the sky, and the stars gathered like drops of glory sinking through the vault of night, and the trees about the churchyard grew black, and Lilith almost vanished in the wide darkness. At length she lifted her head, and seeing the night around her, gave a little broken cry of dismay. The minutes had swept over her head, not through her mind, and she did not know that the dark had come.

"Hearing her cry, Karl rose and approached her. She heard his footsteps, and started to her feet. Karl spoke--

"'Do not be frightened,' he said. 'Let me see you home. I will walk behind you.'

"'Who are you?' she rejoined.

"'Karl Wolkenlicht.'

"'I have heard of you. Thank you. I can go home alone.'

"Yet, as if in a half-dreamy, half-unconscious mood, she accepted his offered hand to lead her through the graves, and allowed him to walk beside her, till, reaching the corner of a narrow street, she suddenly bade him good-night and vanished. He thought it better not to follow her, so he returned her good-night and went home.

"How to see her again was his first thought the next day; as, in fact, how to see her at all had been his first thought for many days. She went nowhere that ever he heard of; she knew nobody that he knew; she was never seen at church, or at market; never seen in the street. Her home had a dreary, desolate aspect. It looked as if no one ever went out or in. It was like a place on which decay had fallen because there was no indwelling spirit. The mud of years was baked upon its door, and no faces looked out of its dusty windows.

"How then could she be the most celebrated beauty of Prague? How then was it that Heinrich Hoellenrachen knew her the moment he saw her? Above all, how was it that Karl Wolkenlicht had, in fact, fallen in love with her before ever he saw her? It was thus--

"Her father was a painter. Belonging thus to the public, it had taken the liberty of re-naming him. Every one called him Teufelsbuerst, or Devilsbrush. It was a name with which, to judge from the nature of his representations, he could hardly fail to be pleased. For, not as a nightmare dream, which may alternate with the loveliest visions, but as his ordinary everyday work, he delighted to represent human suffering.

"Not an aspect of human woe or torture, as expressed in countenance or limb, came before his willing imagination, but he bore it straightway to his easel. In the moments that precede sleep, when the black space before the eyes of the poet teems with lovely faces, or dawns into a spirit-landscape, face after face of suffering, in all varieties of expression, would crowd, as if compelled by the accompanying fiends, to present themselves, in awful levee, before the inner eye of the expectant master. Then he would rise, light his lamp, and, with rapid hand, make notes of his visions; recording, with swift successive sweeps of his pencil, every individual face which had rejoiced his evil fancy. Then he would return to his couch, and, well satisfied, fall asleep to dream yet further embodiments of human ill.

"What wrong could man or mankind have done him, to be thus fearfully pursued by the vengeance of the artist's hate?

"Another characteristic of the faces and form which he drew was, that they were all beautiful in the original idea. The lines of each face, however distorted by pain, would have been, in rest, absolutely beautiful; and the whole of the execution bore witness to the fact that upon this original beauty the painter had directed the artillery of anguish to bring down the sky-soaring heights of its divinity to the level of a hated existence. To do this, he worked in perfect accordance with artistic law, falsifying no line of the original forms. It was the suffering, rather than his pencil, that wrought the change. The latter was the willing instrument to record what the imagination conceived with a cruelty composed enough to be correct.

"To enhance the beauty he had thus distorted, and so to enhance yet further the suffering that produced the distortion, he would often represent attendant demons, whom he made as ugly as his imagination could compass; avoiding, however, all grotesqueness beyond what was sufficient to indicate that they were demons, and not men. Their ugliness rose from hate, envy, and all evil passions; amongst which he especially delighted to represent a gloating exultation over human distress. And often in the midst of his clouds of demon faces, would some one who knew him recognise the painter's own likeness, such as the mirror might have presented it to him when he was busiest over the incarnation of some exquisite torture.

"But apparently with the wish to avoid being supposed to choose such representations for their own sakes, he always found a story, often in the histories of the church, whose name he gave to the painting, and which he pretended to have inspired the pictorial conception. No one, however, who looked upon his suffering martyrs, could suppose for a moment that he honoured their martyrdom. They were but the vehicles for his hate of humanity. He was the torturer, and not Diocletian or Nero.

"But, stranger yet to tell, there was no picture, whatever its subject, into which he did not introduce one form of placid and harmonious loveliness. In this, however, his fierceness was only more fully displayed. For in no case did this form manifest any relation either to the actors or the endurers in the picture. Hence its very loveliness became almost hateful to those who beheld it. Not a shade crossed the still sky of that brow, not a ripple disturbed the still sea of that cheek. She did not hate, she did not love the sufferers: the painter would not have her hate, for that would be to the injury of her loveliness: would not have her love, for he hated. Sometimes she floated above, as a still, unobservant angel, her gaze turned upward, dreaming along, careless as a white summer cloud, across the blue. If she looked down on the scene below, it was only that the beholder might see that she saw and did not care--that not a feather of her outspread pinions would quiver at the sight. Sometimes she would stand in the crowd, as if she had been copied there from another picture, and had nothing to do with this one, nor any right to be in it at all. Or when the red blood was trickling drop by drop from the crushed limb, she might be seen standing nearest, smiling over a primrose or the bloom on a peach. Some had said that she was the painter's wife; that she had been false to him; that he had killed her; and, finding that that was no sufficing revenge, thus half in love, and half in deepest hate, immortalized his vengeance. But it was now universally understood that it was his daughter, of whose loveliness extravagant reports went abroad; though all said, doubtless reading this from her father's pictures, that she was a beauty without a heart. Strange theories of something else supplying its place were rife among the anatomical students. With the girl in the pictures, the wild imagination of Lottchen, probably in part from her apparently absolute unattainableness and her undisputed heartlessness, had fallen in love, as far as the mere imagination can fall in love.

"But again, how was he to see her? He haunted the house night after night. Those blue eyes never met his. No step responsive to his came from that door. It seemed to have been so long unopened that it had grown as fixed and hard as the stones that held its bolts in their passive clasp. He dared not watch in the daytime, and with all his watching at night, he never saw father or daughter or domestic cross the threshold. Little he thought that, from a shot-window near the door, a pair of blue eyes, like Lilith's, but paler and colder, were watching him just as a spider watches the fly that is likely ere long to fall into his toils. And into those toils Karl soon fell. For her form darkened the page; her form stood on the threshold of sleep; and when, overcome with watching, he did enter its precincts, her form entered with him, and walked by his side. He must find her; or the world might go to the bottomless pit for him. But how?

"Yes. He would be a painter. Teufelsbuerst would receive him as a humble apprentice. He would grind his colours, and Teufelsbuerst would teach him the mysteries of the science which is the handmaiden of art. Then he might see ***her***, and that was all his ambition.

"In the clear morning light of a day in autumn, when the leaves were beginning to fall seared from the hand of that Death which has his dance in the chapels of nature as well as in the cathedral aisles of men--he walked up and knocked at the dingy door. The spider painter opened it himself. He was a little man, meagre and pallid, with those faded blue eyes, a low nose in three distinct divisions, and thin, curveless, cruel lips. He wore no hair on his face; but long grey locks, long as a woman's, were scattered over his shoulders, and hung down on his breast. When Wolkenlicht had explained his errand, he smiled a smile in which hypocrisy could not hide the cunning, and, after many difficulties, consented to receive him as a pupil, on condition that he would become an inmate of his house. Wolkenlicht's heart bounded with delight, which he tried to hide: the second smile of Teufelsbuerst might have shown him that he had ill succeeded. The fact that he was not a native of Prague, but coming from a distant part of the country, was entirely his own master in the city, rendered this condition perfectly easy to fulfil; and that very afternoon he entered the studio of Teufelsbuerst as his scholar and servant.

"It was a great room, filled with the appliances and results of art. Many pictures, festooned with cobwebs, were hung carelessly on the dirty walls. Others, half finished, leaned against them, on the floor. Several, in different stages of progress, stood upon easels. But all spoke the cruel bent of the artist's genius. In one corner a lay figure was extended on a couch, covered with a pall of black velvet. Through its folds, the form beneath was easily discernible; and one hand and forearm protruded from beneath it, at right angles to the rest of the frame. Lottchen could not help shuddering when he saw it. Although he overcame the feeling in a moment, he felt a great repugnance to seating himself with his back towards it, as the arrangement of an easel, at which Teufelsbuerst wished him to draw, rendered necessary. He contrived to edge himself round, so that when he lifted his eyes he should see the figure, and be sure that it could not rise without his being aware of it. But his master saw and understood his altered position; and under some pretence about the light, compelled him to resume the position in which he had placed him at first; after which he sat watching, over the top of his picture, the expression of his countenance as he tried to draw; reading in it the horrid fancy that the figure under the pall had risen, and was stealthily approaching to look over his shoulder. But Lottchen resisted the feeling, and, being already no contemptible draughtsman, was soon interested enough to forget it. And then, any moment ***she*** might enter.

"Now began a system of slow torture, for the chance of which the painter had been long on the watch--especially since he had first seen Karl lingering about the house. His opportunities of seeing physical suffering were nearly enough even for the diseased necessities of his art; but now he had one in his power, on whom, his own will fettering him, he could try any experiments he pleased for the production of a kind of suffering, in the observation of which he did not consider that he had yet sufficient experience. He would hold the very heart of the youth in his hand, and wring it and torture it to his own content. And lest Karl should be strong enough to prevent those expressions of pain for which he lay on the watch, he would make use of further means, known to himself, and known to few besides.

"All that day Karl saw nothing of Lilith; but he heard her voice once--and that was enough for one day. The next, she was sitting to her father the greater part of the day, and he could see her as often as he dared glance up from his drawing. She had looked at him when she entered, but had shown no sign of recognition; and all day long she took no further notice of him. He hoped, at first, that this came of the intelligence of love; but he soon began to doubt it. For he saw that, with the holy shadow of sorrow, all that distinguished the expression of her countenance from that which the painter so constantly reproduced, had vanished likewise. It was the very face of the unheeding angel whom, as often as he lifted his eyes higher than hers, he saw on the wall above her, playing on a psaltery in the smoke of the torment ascending for ever from burning Babylon.--The power of the painter had not merely wrought for the representation of the woman of his imagination; it had had scope as well in realizing her.

"Karl soon began to see that communication, other than of the eyes, was all but hopeless; and to any attempt in that way she seemed altogether indisposed to respond. Nor if she had wished it, would it have been safe; for as often as he glanced towards her, instead of hers, he met the blue eyes of the painter gleaming upon him like winter lightning. His tones, his gestures, his words, seemed kind: his glance and his smile refused to be disguised.

"The first day he dined alone in the studio, waited upon by an old woman; the next he was admitted to the family table, with Teufelsbuerst and Lilith. The room offered a strange contrast to the study. As far as handicraft, directed by a sumptuous taste, could construct a house- paradise, this was one. But it seemed rather a paradise of demons; for the walls were covered with Teufelsbuerst's paintings. During the dinner, Lilith's gaze scarcely met that of Wolkenlicht; and once or twice, when their eyes did meet, her glance was so perfectly unconcerned, that Karl wished he might look at her for ever without the fear of her looking at him again. She seemed like one whose love had rushed out glowing with seraphic fire, to be frozen to death in a more than wintry cold: she now walked lonely without her love. In the evenings, he was expected to continue his drawing by lamplight; and at night he was conducted by Teufelsbuerst to his chamber. Not once did he allow him to proceed thither alone, and not once did he leave him there without locking and bolting the door on the outside. But he felt nothing except the coldness of Lilith.

"Day after day she sat to her father, in every variety of costume that could best show the variety of her beauty. How much greater that beauty might be, if it ever blossomed into a beauty of soul, Wolkenlicht never imagined; for he soon loved her enough to attribute to her all the possibilities of her face as actual possessions of her being. To account for everything that seemed to contradict this perfection, his brain was prolific in inventions; till he was compelled at last to see that she was in the condition of a rose-bud, which, on the point of blossoming, had been chilled into a changeless bud by the cold of an untimely frost. For one day, after the father and daughter had become a little more accustomed to his silent presence, a conversation began between them, which went on until he saw that Teufelsbuerst believed in nothing except his art. How much of his feeling for that could be dignified by the name of belief, seeing its objects were such as they were, might have been questioned. It seemed to Wolkenlicht to amount only to this: that, amidst a thousand distastes, it was a pleasant thing to reproduce on the canvas the forms he beheld around him, modifying them to express the prevailing feelings of his own mind.

"A more desolate communication between souls than that which then passed between father and daughter could hardly be imagined. The father spoke of humanity and all its experiences in a tone of the bitterest scorn. He despised men, and himself amongst them; and rejoiced to think that the generations rose and vanished, brood after brood, as the crops of corn grew and disappeared. Lilith, who listened to it all unmoved, taking only an intellectual interest in the question, remarked that even the corn had more life than that; for, after its death, it rose again in the new crop. Whether she meant that the corn was therefore superior to man, forgetting that the superior can produce being without losing its own, or only advanced an objection to her father's argument, Wolkenlicht could not tell. But Teufelsbuerst laughed like the sound of a saw, and said: 'Follow out the analogy, my Lilith, and you will see that man is like the corn that springs again after it is buried; but unfortunately the only result we know of is a vampire.'

"Wolkenlicht looked up, and saw a shudder pass through the frame, and over the pale thin face of the painter. This he could not account for. But Teufelsbuerst could have explained it, for there were strange whispers abroad, and they had reached his ear; and his philosophy was not quite enough for them. But the laugh with which Lilith met this frightful attempt at wit, grated dreadfully on Wolkenlicht's feeling. With her, too, however, a reaction seemed to follow. For, turning round a moment after, and looking at the picture on which her father was working, the tears rose in her eyes, and she said: 'Oh! father, how like my mother you have made me this time!' 'Child!' retorted the painter with a cold fierceness, 'you have no mother. That which is gone out is gone out. Put no name in my hearing on that which is not. Where no substance is, how can there be a name?'

"Lilith rose and left the room. Wolkenlicht now understood that Lilith was a frozen bud, and could not blossom into a rose. But pure love lives by faith. It loves the vaguely beheld and unrealized ideal. It dares believe that the loved is not all that she ever seemed. It is in virtue of this that love loves on. And it was in virtue of this, that Wolkenlicht loved Lilith yet more after he discovered what a grave of misery her unbelief was digging for her within her own soul. For her sake he would bear anything--bear even with calmness the torments of his own love; he would stay on, hoping and hoping.--The text, that we know not what a day may bring forth, is just as true of good things as of evil things; and out of Time's womb the facts must come.

"But with the birth of this resolution to endure, his suffering abated; his face grew more calm; his love, no less earnest, was less imperious; and he did not look up so often from his work when Lilith was present. The master could see that his pupil was more at ease, and that he was making rapid progress in his art. This did not suit his designs, and he would betake himself to his further schemes.

"For this purpose he proceeded first to simulate a friendship for Wolkenlicht, the manifestations of which he gradually increased, until, after a day or two, he asked him to drink wine with him in the evening. Karl readily agreed. The painter produced some of his best; but took care not to allow Lilith to taste it; for he had cunningly prepared and mingled with it a decoction of certain herbs and other ingredients, exercising specific actions upon the brain, and tending to the inordinate excitement of those portions of it which are principally under the rule of the imagination. By the reaction of the brain during the operation of these stimulants, the imagination is filled with suggestions and images. The nature of these is determined by the prevailing mood of the time. They are such as the imagination would produce of itself, but increased in number and intensity. Teufelsbuerst, without philosophizing about it, called his preparation simply a love-philtre, a concoction well known by name, but the composition of which was the secret of only a few. Wolkenlicht had, of course, not the least suspicion of the treatment to which he was subjected.

"Teufelsbuerst was, however, doomed to fresh disappointment. Not that his potion failed in the anticipated effect, for now Karl's real sufferings began; but that such was the strength of Karl's will, and his fear of doing anything that might give a pretext for banishing him from the presence of Lilith, that he was able to conceal his feelings far too successfully for the satisfaction of Teufelsbuerst's art. Yet he had to fetter himself with all the restraints that self-exhortation could load him with, to refrain from falling at the feet of Lilith and kissing the hem of her garment. For that, as the lowliest part of all that surrounded her, itself kissing the earth, seemed to come nearest within the reach of his ambition, and therefore to draw him the most.

"No doubt the painter had experience and penetration enough to perceive that he was suffering intensely; but he wanted to see the suffering embodied in outward signs, bringing it within the region over which his pencil held sway. He kept on, therefore, trying one thing after another, and rousing the poor youth to agony; till to his other sufferings were added, at length, those of failing health; a fact which notified itself evidently enough even for Teufelsbuerst, though its signs were not of the sort he chiefly desired. But Karl endured all bravely.

"Meantime, for various reasons, he scarcely ever left the house.

"I must now interrupt the course of my story to introduce another element.

"A few years before the period of my tale, a certain shoemaker of the city had died under circumstances more than suggestive of suicide. He was buried, however, with such precautions, that six weeks elapsed before the rumour of the facts broke out; upon which rumour, not before, the most fearful reports began to be circulated, supported by what seemed to the people of Prague incontestable evidence.--A ***spectrum*** of the deceased appeared to multitudes of persons, playing horrible pranks, and occasioning indescribable consternation throughout the whole town. This went on till at last, about eight months after his burial, the magistrates caused his body to be dug up; when it was found in just the condition of the bodies of those who in the eastern countries of Europe are called ***vampires***. They buried the corpse under the gallows; but neither the digging up nor the re-burying were of avail to banish the spectre. Again the spade and pick-axe were set to work, and the dead man being found considerably improved in ***condition*** since his last interment, was, with various horrible indignities, burnt to ashes, 'after which the ***spectrum*** was never seen more.'

"And a second epidemic of the same nature had broken out a little before the period to which I have brought my story.

"About midnight, after a calm frosty day, for it was now winter, a terrible storm of wind and snow came on. The tempest howled frightfully about the house of the painter, and Wolkenlicht found some solace in listening to the uproar, for his troubled thoughts would not allow him to sleep. It raged on all the next three days, till about noon on the fourth day, when it suddenly fell, and all was calm. The following night, Wolkenlicht, lying awake, heard unaccountable noises in the next house, as of things thrown about, of kicking and fighting horses, and of opening and shutting gates. Flinging wide his lattice and looking out, the noise of howling dogs came to him from every quarter of the town. The moon was bright and the air was still. In a little while he heard the sounds of a horse going at full gallop round the house, so that it shook as if it would fall; and flashes of light shone into his room. How much of this may have been owing to the effect of the drugs on poor Lottchen's brain, I leave my readers to determine. But when the family met at breakfast in the morning, Teufelsbuerst, who had been already out of doors, reported that he had found the marks of strange feet in the snow, all about the house and through the garden at the back; stating, as his belief, that the tracks must be continued over the roofs, for there was no passage otherwise. There was a wicked gleam in his eye as he spoke; and Lilith believed that he was only trying an experiment on Karl's nerves. He persisted that he had never seen any footprints of the sort before. Karl informed him of his experiences during the night; upon which Teufelsbuerst looked a little graver still, and proceeded to tell them that the storm, whose snow was still covering the ground, had arisen the very moment that their next door neighbour died, and had ceased as suddenly the moment he was buried, though it had raved furiously all the time of the funeral, so that 'it made men's bodies quake and their teeth chatter in their heads.' Karl had heard that the man, whose name was John Kuntz, was dead and buried. He knew that he had been a very wealthy, and therefore most respectable, alderman of the town; that he had been very fond of horses; and that he had died in consequence of a kick received from one of his own, as he was looking at his hoof. But he had not heard that, just before he died, a black cat 'opened the casement with her nails, ran to his bed, and violently scratched his face and the bolster, as if she endeavoured by force to remove him out of the place where he lay. But the cat afterwards was suddenly gone, and she was no sooner gone, but he breathed his last.'

"So said Teufelsbuerst, as the reporter of the town talk. Lilith looked very pale and terrified; and it was perhaps owing to this that the painter brought no more tales home with him. There were plenty to bring, but he heard them all and said nothing. The fact was that the philosopher himself could not resist the infection of the fear that was literally raging in the city; and perhaps the reports that he himself had sold himself to the devil had sufficient response from his own evil conscience to add to the influence of the epidemic upon him. The whole place was infested with the presence of the dead Kuntz, till scarce a man or woman would dare to be alone. He strangled old men; insulted women; squeezed children to death; knocked out the brains of dogs against the ground; pulled up posts; turned milk into blood; nearly killed a worthy clergyman by breathing upon him the intolerable airs of the grave, cold and malignant and noisome; and, in short, filled the city with a perfect madness of fear, so that every report was believed without the smallest doubt or investigation.

"Though Teufelsbuerst brought home no more of the town talk, the old servant was a faithful purveyor, and frequented the news-mart assiduously. Indeed she had some nightmare experiences of her own that she was proud to add to the stock of horrors which the city enjoyed with such a hearty community of goods. For those regions were not far removed from the birthplace and home of the vampire. The belief in vampires is the quintessential concentration and embodiment of all the passion of fear in Hungary and the adjacent regions. Nor, of all the other inventions of the human imagination, has there ever been one so perfect in crawling terror as this. Lilith and Karl were quite familiar with the popular ideas on the subject. It did not require to be explained to them, that a vampire was a body retaining a kind of animal life after the soul had departed. If any relation existed between it and the vanished ghost, it was only sufficient to make it restless in its grave. Possessed of vitality enough to keep it uncorrupted and pliant, its only instinct was a blind hunger for the sole food which could keep its awful life persistent--living human blood. Hence it, or, if not it, a sort of semi-material exhalation or essence of it, retaining its form and material relations, crept from its tomb, and went roaming about till it found some one asleep, towards whom it had an attraction, founded on old affection. It sucked the blood of this unhappy being, transferring so much of its life to itself as a vampire could assimilate. Death was the certain consequence. If suspicion conjectured aright, and they opened the proper grave, the body of the vampire would be found perfectly fresh and plump, sometimes indeed of rather florid complexion;--with grown hair, eyes half open, and the stains of recent blood about its greedy, leech-like lips. Nothing remained but to consume the corpse to ashes, upon which the vampire would show itself no more. But what added infinitely to the horror was the certainty that whoever died from the mouth of the vampire, wrinkled grandsire or delicate maiden, must in turn rise from the grave, and go forth a vampire, to suck the blood of the dearest left behind. This was the generation of the vampire brood. Lilith trembled at the very name of the creature. Karl was too much in love to be afraid of anything. Yet the evident fear of the unbelieving painter took a hold of his imagination; and, under the influence of the potions of which he still partook unwittingly, when he was not thinking about Lilith, he was thinking about the vampire.

"Meantime, the condition of things in the painter's household continued much the same for Wolkenlicht--work all day; no communication between the young people; the dinner and the wine; silent reading when work was done, with stolen glances many over the top of the book, glances that were never returned; the cold good-night; the locking of the door; the wakeful night and the drowsy morning. But at length a change came, and sooner than any of the party had expected. For, whether it was that the impatience of Teufelsbuerst had urged him to yet more dangerous experiments, or that the continuance of those he had been so long employing had overcome at length the vitality of Wolkenlicht--one afternoon, as he was sitting at his work, he suddenly dropped from his chair, and his master hurrying to him in some alarm, found him rigid and apparently lifeless. Lilith was not in the study when this took place. In justice to Teufelsbuerst, it must be confessed that he employed all the skill he was master of, which for beneficent purposes was not very great, to restore the youth; but without avail. At last, hearing the footsteps of Lilith, he desisted in some consternation; and that she might escape being shocked by the sight of a dead body where she had been accustomed to see a living one, he removed the lay figure from the couch, and laid Karl in its place, covering him with a black velvet pall. He was just in time. She started at seeing no one in Karl's place and said:

"'Where is your pupil, father?'

"'Gone home,' he answered, with a kind of convulsive grin.

"She glanced round the room, caught sight of the lay figure where it had not been before, looked at the couch, and saw the pall yet heaved up from beneath, opened her eyes till the entire white sweep around the iris suggested a new expression of consternation to Teufelsbuerst, though from a quarter whence he did not desire or look for it; and then, without a word, sat down to a drawing she had been busy upon the day before. But her father, glancing at her now, as Wolkenlicht had used to do, could not help seeing that she was frightfully pale. She showed no other sign of uneasiness. As soon as he released her, she withdrew, with one more glance, as she passed, at the couch and the figure blocked out in black upon it. She hastened to her chamber, shut and locked the door, sat down on the side of the couch, and fell, not a-weeping, but a-thinking. Was he dead? What did it matter? They would all be dead soon. Her mother was dead already. It was only that the earth could not bear more children, except she devoured those to whom she had already given birth. But what if they had to come back in another form, and live another sad, hopeless, loveless life over again?--And so she went on questioning, and receiving no replies; while through all her thoughts passed and repassed the eyes of Wolkenlicht, which she had often felt to be upon her when she did not see them, wild with repressed longing, the light of their love shining through the veil of diffused tears, ever gathering and never overflowing. Then came the pale face, so worshipping, so distant in its self-withdrawn devotion, slowly dawning out of the vapours of her reverie. When it vanished, she tried to see it again. It would not come when she called it; but when her thoughts left knocking at the door of the lost, and wandered away, out came the pale, troubled, silent face again, gathering itself up from some unknown nook in her world of phantasy, and once more, when she tried to steady it by the fixedness of her own regard, fading back into the mist. So the phantasm of the dead drew near and wooed, as the living had never dared.--What if there were any good in loving? What if men and women did not die all out, but some dim shade of each, like that pale, mind-ghost of Wolkenlicht, floated through the eternal vapours of chaos? And what if they might sometimes cross each other's path, meet, know that they met, love on? Would not that revive the withered memory, fix the fleeting ghost, give a new habitation, a body even, to the poor, unhoused wanderers, frozen by the eternal frosts, no longer thinking beings, but thoughts wandering through the brain of the 'Melancholy Mass?' Back with the thought came the face of the dead Karl, and the maiden threw herself on her bed in a flood of bitter tears. She could have loved him if he had only lived: she did love him, for he was dead. But even in the midst of the remorse that followed--for had she not killed him?--life seemed a less hard and hopeless thing than before. For it is love itself and not its responses or results that is the soul of life and its pleasures.

"Two hours passed ere she could again show herself to her father, from whom she seemed in some new way divided by the new feeling in which he did not, and could not share. But at last, lest he should seek her, and finding her, should suspect her thoughts, she descended and sought him.-- For there is a maidenliness in sorrow, that wraps her garments close around her.--But he was not to be seen; the door of the study was locked. A shudder passed through her as she thought of what her father, who lost no opportunity of furthering his all but perfect acquaintance with the human form and structure, might be about with the figure which she knew lay dead beneath that velvet pall, but which had arisen to haunt the hollow caves and cells of her living brain. She rushed away, and up once more to her silent room, through the darkness which had now settled down in the house; threw herself again on her bed, and lay almost paralysed with horror and distress.

"But Teufelsbuerst was not about anything so frightful as she supposed, though something frightful enough. I have already implied that Wolkenlicht was, in form, as fine an embodiment of youthful manhood as any old Greek republic could have provided one of its sculptors with as model for an Apollo. It is true, that to the eye of a Greek artist he would not have been more acceptable in consequence of the regimen he had been going through for the last few weeks; but the emaciation of Wolkenlicht's frame, and the consequent prominence of the muscles, indicating the pain he had gone through, were peculiarly attractive to Teufelsbuerst.--He was busy preparing to take a cast of the body of his dead pupil, that it might aid to the perfection of his future labours.

"He was deep in the artistic enjoyment of a form, at the same time so beautiful and strong, yet with the lines of suffering in every limb and feature, when his daughter's hand was laid on the latch. He started, flung the velvet drapery over the body, and went to the door. But Lilith had vanished. He returned to his labours. The operation took a long time, for he performed it very carefully. Towards midnight, he had finished encasing the body in a close-clinging shell of plaster, which, when broken off, and fitted together, would be the matrix to the form of the dead Wolkenlicht. Before leaving it to harden till the morning, he was just proceeding to strengthen it with an additional layer all over, when a flash of lightning, reflected in all its dazzle from the snow without, almost blinded him. A peal of long-drawn thunder followed; the wind rose; and just such a storm came on as had risen some time before at the death of Kuntz, whose spectre was still tormenting the city. The gnomes of terror, deep hidden in the caverns of Teufelsbuerst's nature, broke out jubilant. With trembling hands he tried to cast the pall over the awful white chrysalis,--failed, and fled to his chamber. And there lay the studio naked to the eyes of the lightning, with its tortured forms throbbing out of the dark, and quivering, as with life, in the almost continuous palpitations of the light; while on the couch lay the motionless mass of whiteness, gleaming blue in the lightning, almost more terrible in its crude indications of the human form, than that which it enclosed. It lay there as if dropped from some tree of chaos, haggard with the snows of eternity--a huge misshapen nut, with a corpse for its kernel.

"But the lightning would soon have revealed a more terrible sight still, had there been any eyes to behold it. At midnight, while a peal of thunder was just dying away in the distance, the crust of death flew asunder, rending in all directions; and, pale as his investiture, staring with ghastly eyes, the form of Karl started up sitting on the couch. Had he not been far beyond ordinary men in strength, he could not thus have rent his sepulchre. Indeed, had Teufelsbuerst been able to finish his task by the additional layer of gypsum which he contemplated, he must have died the moment life revived; although, so long as the trance lasted, neither the exclusion from the air, nor the practical solidification of the walls of his chest, could do him any injury. He had lain unconscious throughout the operations of Teufelsbuerst, but now the catalepsy had passed away, possibly under the influence of the electric condition of the atmosphere. Very likely the strength he now put forth was intensified by a convulsive reaction of all the powers of life, as is not infrequently the case in sudden awakenings from similar interruptions of vital activity. The coming to himself and the bursting of his case were simultaneous. He sat staring about him, with, of all his mental faculties, only his imagination awake, from which the thoughts that occupied it when he fell senseless had not yet faded. These thoughts had been compounded of feelings about Lilith, and speculations about the vampire that haunted the neighbourhood; and the fumes of the last drug of which he had partaken, still hovering in his brain, combined with these thoughts and fancies to generate the delusion that he had just broken from the embrace of his coffin, and risen, the last-born of the vampire race. The sense of unavoidable obligation to fulfil his doom, was yet mingled with a faint flutter of joy, for he knew that he must go to Lilith. With a deep sigh, he rose, gathered up the pall of black velvet, flung it around him, stepped from the couch, and left the study to find her.

"Meantime, Teufelsbuerst had sufficiently recovered to remember that he had left the door of the studio unfastened, and that any one entering would discover in what he had been engaged, which, in the case of his getting into any difficulty about the death of Karl, would tell powerfully against him. He was at the farther end of a long passage, leading from the house to the studio, on his way to make all secure, when Karl appeared at the door, and advanced towards him. The painter, seized with invincible terror, turned and fled. He reached his room, and fell senseless on the floor. The phantom held on its way, heedless.

"Lilith, on gaining her room the second time, had thrown herself on her bed as before, and had wept herself into a troubled slumber. She lay dreaming--and dreadful dreams. Suddenly she awoke in one of those peals of thunder which tormented the high regions of the air, as a storm billows the surface of the ocean. She lay awake and listened. As it died away, she thought she heard, mingling with its last muffled murmurs, the sound of moaning. She turned her face towards the room in keen terror. But she saw nothing. Another light, long-drawn sigh reached her ear, and at the same moment a flash of lightning illumined the room. In the corner farthest from her bed, she spied a white face, nothing more. She was dumb and motionless with fear. Utter darkness followed, a darkness that seemed to enter into her very brain. Yet she felt that the face was slowly crossing the black gulf of the room, and drawing near to where she lay. The next flash revealed, as it bended over her, the ghastly face of Karl, down which flowed fresh tears. The rest of his form was lost in blackness. Lilith did not faint, but it was the very force of her fear that seemed to keep her alive. It became for the moment the atmosphere of her life. She lay trembling and staring at the spot in the darkness where she supposed the face of Karl still to be. But the next flash showed her the face far off, looking at her through the panes of her lattice-window.

"For Lottchen, as soon as he saw Lilith, seemed to himself to go through a second stage of awaking. Her face made him doubt whether he could be a vampire after all; for instead of wanting to bite her arm and suck the blood, he all but fell down at her feet in a passion of speechless love. The next moment he became aware that his presence must be at least very undesirable to her; and in an instant he had reached her window, which he knew looked upon a lower roof that extended between two different parts of the house, and before the next flash came, he had stepped through the lattice and closed it behind him.

"Believing his own room to be attainable from this quarter, he proceeded along the roof in the direction he judged best. The cold winter air by degrees restored him entirely to his right mind, and he soon comprehended the whole of the circumstances in which he found himself. Peeping through a window he was passing, to see whether it belonged to his room, he spied Teufelsbuerst, who, at the very moment, was lifting his head from the faint into which he had fallen at the first sight of Lottchen. The moon was shining clear, and in its light the painter saw, to his horror, the pale face staring in at his window. He thought it had been there ever since he had fainted, and dropped again in a deeper swoon than before. Karl saw him fall, and the truth flashed upon him that the wicked artist took him for what he had believed himself to be when first he recovered from his trance--namely, the vampire of the former Karl Wolkenlicht. The moment he comprehended it, he resolved to keep up the delusion if possible. Meantime he was innocently preparing a new ingredient for the popular dish of horrors to be served at the ordinary of the city the next day. For the old servant's were not the only eyes that had seen him besides those of Teufelsbuerst. What could be more like a vampire, dragging his pall after him, than this apparition of poor, half-frozen Lottchen, crawling across the roof? Karl remembered afterwards that he had heard the dogs howling awfully in every direction, as he crept along; but this was hardly necessary to make those who saw him conclude that it was the same phantasm of John Kuntz, which had been infesting the whole city, and especially the house next door to the painter's, which had been the dwelling of the respectable alderman who had degenerated into this most disreputable of moneyless vagabonds. What added to the consternation of all who heard of it, was the sickening conviction that the extreme measures which they had resorted to in order to free the city from the ghoul, beyond which nothing could be done, had been utterly unavailing, successful as they had proved in every other known case of the kind. For, urged as well by various horrid signs about his grave, which not even its close proximity to the altar could render a place of repose, they had opened it, had found in the body every peculiarity belonging to a vampire, had pulled it out with the greatest difficulty on account of a quite supernatural ponderosity; which rendered the horse which had killed him--a strong animal--all but unable to drag it along, and had at last, after cutting it in pieces, and expending on the fire two hundred and sixteen great billets, succeeded in conquering its incombustibleness, and reducing it to ashes. Such, at least, was the story which had reached the painter's household, and was believed by many; and if all this did not compel the perturbed corpse to rest, what more could be done?

"When Karl had reached his room, and was dressing himself, the thought struck him that something might be made of the report of the extreme weight of the body of old Kuntz, to favour the continuance of the delusion of Teufelsbuerst, although he hardly knew yet to what use he could turn this delusion. He was convinced that he would have made no progress however long he might have remained in his house; and that he would have more chance of favour with Lilith if he were to meet her in any other circumstances whatever than those in which he invariably saw her--namely, surrounded by her father's influences, and watched by her father's cold blue eyes.

"As soon as he was dressed, he crept down to the studio, which was now quiet enough, the storm being over, and the moon filling it with her steady shine. In the corner lay in all directions the fragments of the mould which his own body had formed and filled. The bag of plaster and the bucket of water which the painter had been using stood beside. Lottchen gathered all the pieces together, and then making his way to an outhouse where he had seen various odds and ends of rubbish lying, chose from the heap as many pieces of old iron and other metal as he could find. To these he added a few large stones from the garden. When he had got all into the studio, he locked the door, and proceeded to fit together the parts of the mould, filling up the hollow as he went on with the heaviest things he could get into it, and solidifying the whole by pouring in plaster; till, having at length completed it, and obliterated, as much as possible, the marks of joining, he left it to harden, with the conviction that now it would make a considerable impression on Teufelsbuerst's imagination, as well as on his muscular sense. He then left everything else as nearly undisturbed as he could; and, knowing all the ways of the house, was soon in the street, without leaving any signs of his exit.

"Karl soon found himself before the house in which his friend Hoellenrachen resided. Knowing his studious habits, he had hoped to see his light still burning, nor was he disappointed. He contrived to bring him to his window, and a moment after, the door was cautiously opened.

"'Why, Lottchen, where do you come from?'

"'From the grave, Heinrich, or next door to it.'

"'Come in, and tell me all about it. We thought the old painter had made a model of you, and tortured you to death.'

"'Perhaps you were not far wrong. But get me a horn of ale, for even a vampire is thirsty, you know.'

"'A vampire!' exclaimed Heinrich, retreating a pace, and involuntarily putting himself upon his guard.

"Karl laughed.

"'My hand was warm, was it not, old fellow?' he said. Vampires are cold, all but the blood.'

"'What a fool I am!' rejoined Heinrich. 'But you know we have been hearing such horrors lately that a fellow may be excused for shuddering a little when a pale-faced apparition tells him at two o'clock in the morning that he is a vampire, and thirsty, too.'

"Karl told him the whole story; and the mental process of regarding it for the sake of telling it, revealed to him pretty clearly some of the treatment of which he had been unconscious at the time. Heinrich was quite sure that his suspicions were correct. And now the question was, what was to be done next?

"'At all events,' said Heinrich, 'we must keep you out of the way for some time. I will represent to my landlady that you are in hiding from enemies, and her heart will rule her tongue. She can let you have a garret-room, I know; and I will do as well as I can to bear you company. We shall have time then to invent some plan of operation.'

"To this proposal Karl agreed with hearty thanks, and soon all was arranged. The only conclusion they could yet arrive at was, that somehow or other the old demon-painter must be tamed.

"Meantime, how fared it with Lilith? She too had no doubt that she had seen the body-ghost of poor Karl, and that the vampire had, according to rule, paid her the first visit because he loved her best. This was horrible enough if the vampire were not really the person he represented; but if in any sense it were Karl himself, at least it gave some expectation of a more prolonged existence than her father had taught her to look for; and if love anything like her mother's still lasted, even along with the habits of a vampire, there was something to hope for in the future. And then, though he had visited her, he had not, as far as she was aware, deprived her of a drop of blood. She could not be certain that he had not bitten her, for she had been in such a strange condition of mind that she might not have felt it, but she believed that he had restrained the impulses of his vampire nature, and had left her, lest he should yet yield to them. She fell fast asleep; and, when morning came, there was not, as far as she could judge, one of those triangular leech-like perforations to be found upon her whole body. Will it be believed that the moment she was satisfied of this, she was seized by a terrible jealousy, lest Karl should have gone and bitten some one else? Most people will wonder that she should not have gone out of her senses at once; but there was all the difference between a visit from a real vampire and a visit from a man she had begun to love, even although she took him for a vampire. All the difference does ***not*** lie in a name. They were very different causes, and the effects must be very different.

"When Teufelsbuerst came down in the morning, he crept into the studio like a murderer. There lay the awful white block, seeming to his eyes just the same as he had left it. What was to be done with it? He dared not open it. Mould and model must go together. But whither? If inquiry should be made after Wolkenlicht, and this were discovered anywhere on his premises, would it not be enough to bring him at once to the gallows? Therefore it would be dangerous to bury it in the garden, or in the cellar.

"'Besides,' thought he, with a shudder, 'that would be to fix the vampire as a guest for ever.'--And the horrors of the past night rushed back upon his imagination with renewed intensity. What would it be to have the dead Karl crawling about his house for ever, now inside, now out, now sitting on the stairs, now staring in at the windows?

"He would have dragged it to the bottom of his garden, past which the Moldau flowed, and plunged it into the stream; but then, should the spectre continue to prove troublesome, it would be almost impossible to reach the body so as to destroy it by fire; besides which, he could not do it without assistance, and the probability of discovery. If, however, the apparition should turn out to be no vampire, but only a respectable ghost, they might manage to endure its presence, till it should be weary of haunting them.

"He resolved at last to convey the body for the meantime into a concealed cellar in the house, seeing something must be done before his daughter came down. Proceeding to remove it, his consternation as greatly increased when he discovered how the body had grown in weight since he had thus disposed of it, leaving on his mind scarcely a hope that it could turn out not to be a vampire after all. He could scarcely stir it, and there was but one whom he could call to his assistance--the old woman who acted as his housekeeper and servant.

"He went to her room, roused her, and told her the whole story. Devoted to her master for many years, and not quite so sensitive to fearful influences as when less experienced in horrors, she showed immediate readiness to render him assistance. Utterly unable, however, to lift the mass between them, they could only drag and push it along; and such a slow toil was it that there was no time to remove the traces of its track, before Lilith came down and saw a broad white line leading from the door of the studio down the cellar-stairs. She knew in a moment what it meant; but not a word was uttered about the matter, and the name of Karl Wolkenlicht seemed to be entirely forgotten.

"But how could the affairs of a house go on all the same when every one of the household knew that a dead body lay in the cellar?--nay more, that, although it lay still and dead enough all day, it would come half alive at nightfall, and, turning the whole house into a sepulchre by its presence, go creeping about like a cat all over it in the dark--perhaps with phosphorescent eyes? So it was not surprising that the painter abandoned his studio early, and that the three found themselves together in the gorgeous room formerly described, as soon as twilight began to fall.

"Already Teufelsbuerst had begun to experience a kind of shrinking from the horrid faces in his own pictures, and to feel disgusted at the abortions of his own mind. But all that he and the old woman now felt was an increasing fear as the night drew on, a kind of sickening and paralysing terror. The thing down there would not lie quiet--at least its phantom in the cellars of their imagination would not. As much as possible, however, they avoided alarming Lilith, who, knowing all they knew, was as silent as they. But her mind was in a strange state of excitement, partly from the presence of a new sense of love, the pleasure of which all the atmosphere of grief into which it grew could not totally quench. It comforted her somehow, as a child may comfort when his father is away.

"Bedtime came, and no one made a move to go. Without a word spoken on the subject, the three remained together all night; the elders nodding and slumbering occasionally, and Lilith getting some share of repose on a couch. All night the shape of death might be somewhere about the house; but it did not disturb them. They heard no sound, saw no sight; and when the morning dawned, they separated, chilled and stupid, and for the time beyond fear, to seek repose in their private chambers. There they remained equally undisturbed.

"But when the painter approached his easel a few hours after, looking more pale and haggard still than he was wont, from the fears of the night, a new bewilderment took possession of him. He had been busy with a fresh embodiment of his favourite subject, into which he had sketched the form of the student as the sufferer. He had represented poor Wolkenlicht as just beginning to recover from a trance, while a group of surgeons, unaware of the signs of returning life, were absorbed in a minute dissection of one of the limbs. At an open door he had painted Lilith passing, with her face buried in a bunch of sweet peas. But when he came to the picture, he found, to his astonishment and terror, that the face of one of the group was now turned towards that of the victim, regarding his revival with demoniac satisfaction, and taking pains to prevent the others from discovering it. The face of this prince of torturers was that of Teufelsbuerst himself. Lilith had altogether vanished, and in her place stood the dim vampire reiteration of the body that lay extended on the table, staring greedily at the assembled company. With trembling hands the painter removed the picture from the easel, and turned its face to the wall.

"Of course this was the work of Lottchen. When he left the house, he took with him the key of a small private door, which was so seldom used that, while it remained closed, the key would not be missed, perhaps for many months. Watching the windows, he had chosen a safe time to enter, and had been hard at work all night on these alterations. Teufelsbuerst attributed them to the vampire, and left the picture as he found it, not daring to put brush to it again.

"The next night was passed much after the same fashion. But the fear had begun to die away a little in the hearts of the women, who did not know what had taken place in the studio on the previous night. It burrowed, however, with gathered force in the vitals of Teufelsbuerst. But this night likewise passed in peace; and before it was over, the old woman had taken to speculating in her own mind as to the best way of disposing of the body, seeing it was not at all likely to be troublesome. But when the painter entered his studio in trepidation the next morning, he found that the form of the lovely Lilith was painted out of every picture in the room. This could not be concealed; and Lilith and the servant became aware that the studio was the portion of the house in haunting which the vampire left the rest in peace.

"Karl recounted all the tricks he had played to his friend Heinrich, who begged to be allowed to bear him company the following night. To this Karl consented, thinking it would be considerably more agreeable to have a companion. So they took a couple of bottles of wine and some provisions with them, and before midnight found themselves snug in the studio. They sat very quiet for some time, for they knew that if they were seen, two vampires would not be so terrible as one, and might occasion discovery. But at length Heinrich could bear it no longer. "'I say, Lottchen, let's go and look; for your dead body. What has the old beggar done with it?'

"'I think I know. Stop; let me peep out. All right! Come along.'

"With a lamp in his hand, he led the way to the cellars, and after searching about a little they discovered it.

"'It looks horrid enough,' said Heinrich, 'but think a drop or two of wine would brighten it up a little.'

"So he took a bottle from his pocket, and after they had had a glass apiece, he dropped a third in blots all over the plaster. Being red wine, it had the effect Hoellenrachen desired.

"'When they visit it next, they will know that the vampire can find the food he prefers,' said he.

"In a corner close by the plaster, they found the clothes Karl had worn.

"'Hillo!' said Heinrich, 'we'll make something of this find.'

"So he carried them with him to the studio. There he got hold of the lay-figure.

"'What are you about, Heinrich?'

"'Going to make a scarecrow to keep the ravens off old Teufel's pictures,' answered Heinrich, as he went on dressing the lay-figure in Karl's clothes. He next seated the creature at an easel with its back to the door, so that it should be the first thing the painter should see when he entered. Karl meant to remove this before he went, for it was too comical to fall in with the rest of his proceedings. But the two sat down to their supper, and by the time they had finished the wine, they thought they should like to go to bed. So they got up and went home, and Karl forgot the lay-figure, leaving it in busy motionlessness all night before the easel.

"When Teufelsbuerst saw it, he turned and fled with a cry that brought his daughter to his help. He rushed past her, able only to articulate:

"The vampire! The vampire! Painting!'

"Far more courageous than he, because her conscience was more peaceful, Lilith passed on to the studio. She too recoiled a step or two when she saw the figure; but with the sight of the back of Karl, as she supposed it to be, came the longing to see the face that was on the other side. So she crept round and round by the wall, as far off as she could. The figure remained motionless. It was a strange kind of shock that she experienced when she saw the face, disgusting from its inanity. The absurdity next struck her; and with the absurdity flashed into her mind the conviction that this was not the doing of a vampire; for of all creatures under the moon, he could not be expected to be a humorist. A wild hope sprang up in her mind that Karl was not dead. Of this she soon resolved to make herself sure.

"She closed the door of the studio; in the strength of her new hope undressed the figure, put it in its place, concealed the garments--all the work of a few minutes; and then, finding her father just recovering from the worst of his fear, told him there was nothing in the studio but what ought to be there, and persuaded him to go and see. He not only saw no one, but found that no further liberties had been taken with his pictures. Reassured, he soon persuaded himself that the spectre in this case had been the offspring of his own terror-haunted brain. But he had no spirit for painting now. He wandered about the house, himself haunting it like a restless ghost.

"When night came, Lilith retired to her own room. The waters of fear had begun to subside in the house; but the painter and his old attendant did not yet follow her example.

"As soon, however, as the house was quite still, Lilith glided noiselessly down the stairs, went into the studio, where as yet there assuredly was no vampire, and concealed herself in a corner.

"As it would not do for an earnest student like Heinrich to be away from his work very often, he had not asked to accompany Lottchen this time. And indeed Karl himself, a little anxious about the result of the scarecrow, greatly preferred going alone.

"While she was waiting for what might happen, the conviction grew upon Lilith, as she reviewed all the past of the story, that these phenomena were the work of the real Karl, and of no vampire. In a few moments she was still more sure of this. Behind the screen where she had taken refuge, hung one of the pictures out of which her portrait had been painted the night before last. She had taken a lamp with her into the studio, with the intention of extinguishing it the moment she heard any sign of approach; but as the vampire lingered, she began to occupy herself with examining the picture beside her. She had not looked at it long, before she wetted the tip of her forefinger, and began to rub away at the obliteration. Her suspicions were instantly confirmed: the substance employed was only a gummy wash over the paint. The delight she experienced at the discovery threw her into a mischievous humour.

"'I will see,' she said to herself, 'whether I cannot match Karl Wolkenlicht at this game.'

"In a closet in the room hung a number of costumes, which Lilith had at different times worn for her father. Among them was a large white drapery, which she easily disposed as a shroud. With the help of some chalk, she soon made herself ghastly enough, and then placing her lamp on the floor behind the screen, and setting a chair over it, so that it should throw no light in any direction, she waited once more for the vampire. Nor had she much longer to wait. She soon heard a door move, the sound of which she hardly knew, and then the studio door opened. Her heart beat dreadfully, not with fear lest it should be a vampire after all, but with hope that it was Karl. To see him once more was too great joy. Would she not make up to him for all her coldness! But would he care for her now? Perhaps he had been quite cured of his longing for a hard heart like hers. She peeped. It was he sure enough, looking as handsome as ever. He was holding his light to look at her last work, and the expression of his face, even in regarding her handiwork, was enough to let her know that he loved her still. If she had not seen this, she dared not have shown herself from her hiding-place. Taking the lamp in her hand, she got upon the chair, and looked over the screen, letting the light shine from below upon her face. She then made a slight noise to attract Karl's attention. He looked up, evidently rather startled, and saw the face of Lilith in the air. He gave a stifled cry threw himself on his knees with his arms stretched towards her, and moaned--

"'I have killed her! I have killed her!'

"Lilith descended, and approached him noiselessly. He did not move. She came close to him and said--

"'Are you Karl Wolkenlicht?'

"His lips moved, but no sound came.

"'If you are a vampire, and I am a ghost,' she said--but a low happy laugh alone concluded the sentence.

"Karl sprang to his feet. Lilith's laugh changed into a burst of sobbing and weeping, and in another moment the ghost was in the arms of the vampire.

"Lilith had no idea how far her father had wronged Karl, and though, from thinking over the past, he had no doubt that the painter had drugged him, he did not wish to pain her by imparting this conviction. But Lilith was afraid of a reaction of rage and hatred in her father after the terror was removed; and Karl saw that he might thus be deprived of all further intercourse with Lilith, and all chance of softening the old man's heart towards him; while Lilith would not hear of forsaking him who had banished all the human race but herself. They managed at length to agree upon a plan of operation.

"The first thing they did was to go to the cellar where the plaster mass lay, Karl carrying with him a great axe used for cleaving wood. Lilith shuddered when she saw it, stained as it was with the wine Heinrich had spilt over it, and almost believed herself the midnight companion of a vampire after all, visiting with him the terrible corpse in which he lived all day. But Karl soon reassured her; and a few good blows of the axe revealed a very different core to that which Teufelsbuerst supposed to be in it. Karl broke it into pieces, and with Lilith's help, who insisted on carrying her share, the whole was soon at the bottom of the Moldau and every trace of its ever having existed removed. Before morning, too, the form of Lilith had dawned anew in every picture. There was no time to restore to its former condition the one Karl had first altered; for in it the changes were all that they seemed; nor indeed was he capable of restoring it in the master's style; but they put it quite out of the way, and hoped that sufficient time might elapse before the painter thought of it again.

"When they had done, and Lilith, for all his entreaties, would remain with him no longer, Karl took his former clothes with him, and having spent the rest of the night in his old room, dressed in them in the morning. When Teufelsbuerst entered his studio next day, there sat Karl, as if nothing had happened, finishing the drawing on which he had been at work when the fit of insensibility came upon him. The painter started, stared, rubbed his eyes, thought it was another spectral illusion, and was on the point of yielding to his terror, when Karl rose, and approached him with a smile. The healthy, sunshiny countenance of Karl, let him be ghost or goblin, could not fail to produce somewhat of a tranquilizing effect on Teufelsbuerst. He took his offered hand mechanically, his countenance utterly vacant with idiotic bewilderment. Karl said:

"'I was not well, and thought it better to pay a visit to a friend for a few days; but I shall soon make up for lost time, for I am all right now.'

"He sat down at once, taking no notice of his master's behaviour, and went on with his drawing. Teufelsbuerst stood staring at him for some minutes without moving, then suddenly turned and left the room. Karl heard him hurrying down the cellar stairs. In a few moments he came up again. Karl stole a glance at him. There he stood in the same spot, no doubt more full of bewilderment than ever, but it was not possible that his face should express more. At last he went to his easel, and sat down with a long-drawn sigh as if of relief. But though he sat at his easel, he painted none that day; and as often as Karl ventured a glance, he saw him still staring at him. The discovery that his pictures were restored to their former condition aided, no doubt, in leading him to the same conclusion as the other facts, whatever that conclusion might be--probably that he had been the sport of some evil power, and had been for the greater part of a week utterly bewitched. Lilith had taken care to instruct the old woman, with whom she was all-powerful; and as neither of them showed the smallest traces of the astonishment which seemed to be slowly vitrifying his own brain, he was at last perfectly satisfied that things had been going on all right everywhere but in his inner man; and in this conclusion he certainly was not far wrong, in more senses than one. But when all was restored again to the old routine, it became evident that the peculiar direction of his art in which he had hitherto indulged had ceased to interest him. The shock had acted chiefly upon that part of his mental being which had been so absorbed. He would sit for hours without doing anything, apparently plunged in meditation.--Several weeks elapsed without any change, and both Lilith and Karl were getting dreadfully anxious about him. Karl paid him every attention; and the old man, for he now looked much older than before, submitted to receive his services as well as those of Lilith. At length, one morning, he said in a slow thoughtful tone:

"'Karl Wolkenlicht, I should like to paint you.'

"'Certainly, sir,' answered Karl, jumping up, 'where would you like me to sit?'

"So the ice of silence and inactivity was broken, and the painter drew and painted; and the spring of his art flowed once more; and he made a beautiful portrait of Karl--a portrait without evil or suffering. And as soon as he had finished Karl, he began once more to paint Lilith; and when he had painted her, he composed a picture for the very purpose of introducing them together; and in this picture there was neither ugliness nor torture, but human feeling and human hope instead. Then Karl knew that he might speak to him of Lilith; and he spoke, and was heard with a smile. But he did not dare to tell him the truth of the vampire story till one day that Teufelsbuerst was lying on the floor of a room in Karl's ancestral castle, half smothered in grandchildren; when the only answer it drew from the old man was a kind of shuddering laugh and the words--'Don't speak of it, Karl, my boy!'"

* * * * *

No one had interrupted Harry. His brother had put a shovelful of coals on the fire, to keep up the flame; but not a word had been spoken. The cold moon had shone in at the windows all the time, her light made yet colder by the snowy sheen from the face of the earth; and any horror that the story could generate had had full freedom to operate on the minds of the listeners.

"Well, I'm glad its over, for my part," said Mrs. Bloomfield. "It made my flesh creep."

"I do not see any good in founding a story upon a superstition. One knows it is false, all the time," said Mrs. Cathcart.

"But," said Harry, "all that I have related might have taken place; for the story is not founded on the superstition itself, but on the belief of the people of the time in the superstition. I have merely used this belief to give the general tone to the story, and sometimes the particular occasion for events in it, the vampire being a terrible fact to those times."

"You write," said the curate, "as if you quoted occasionally from some authority."

"The story of John Kuntz, as well as that of the shoemaker, is told by Henry More in his ***Antidote against Atheism***. He believed the whole affair. His authority is Martin Weinrich, a Silesian doctor. I have only taken the liberty of shifting the scene of the ***post-mortem*** exploits of Kuntz from a town of Silesia to Prague."

"Well, Harry," said his sister-in-law, "if your object was to frighten us, I confess that I for one was tolerably uncomfortable. But I don't know that that is a very high aim in story-telling."

"If that were all--certainly not," replied Harry, glancing towards Adela, who had not spoken. Nor did she speak yet. But her expression showed plainly enough that it was not the horror of the story that had taken chief hold of her mind. Her face was full of suppressed light, and she was evidently satisfied--or shall I call it ***gratified***?--as well as delighted with the tale. Something or other in it had touched her not only deeply, but nearly.

Nothing was said about another meeting--perhaps because, from Adela's illness, the order had been interrupted, and the present had required a special summons.

The ladies had gone up stairs to put on their bonnets. I had crossed into the library, which was on the same floor with the drawing-room, to find out if I was right in supposing I had seen some volumes of Henry More's works on the shelves--certainly the colonel could never have bought them. Our host, the curate and the schoolmaster had followed me. Harry had remained behind in the drawing-room. Thinking of something I wanted to say to him before he went, I left the gentlemen looking over the book-shelves, and went to cross again to the drawing-room. But when I reached the door, there stood at the top of the stair, Adela and Harry. She had evidently just said something warm about the story. I could almost read what she had said still lingering on her face, which was turned up a good deal to look into his, so near each other were they standing. Hers had a rosy flush as of sunset over it, while his glowed like the sun rising in a mist. Evidently the pleasures of giving and receiving were in this case nearly equal. But they were not of long duration; for the moment I appeared, they bade each other a hurried good night, and parted. I, thinking it better to pretermit my speech to Harry, retreated into the library, and was glad to think that no one had seen that conference but myself. Such a conjunction of planets prefigured, however, not merely warm spring weather, but sultry gloom, and thunderous clouds to follow; and although I was delighted with my astronomical observation, I could not help growing anxious about the omen.

CHAPTER VII.
THE CASTLE.

The next day, as I passed the school-house on my way to call on the curate, I heard such an uproar that I stopped involuntarily to listen. I soon satisfied myself that it was only the usual water-spout occasioned on the ocean of boyhood by the vacuum of the master. As soon as I entered the curate's study, there stood the missing master, hat in hand. He had not sat down, and would not, hearing all the time, no doubt, in his soul, the far confusion of his forsaken realm. He had but that moment entered.

"You come just in the right time, Smith," said the curate.--We had already dropped unnecessary prefixes.--"Here is Mr. Bloomfield come to ask us to spend a final evening with him and Mrs. Bloomfield. And in the name of the whole company, I have taken upon me to assure him that it will give us pleasure. Am I not right?"

"Undoubtedly," I replied. "What evening have you fixed upon, Mr. Bloomfield?"

"This day week," he answered. "Shall I tell you why I put it off so long?"

"If you please."

"I heard your brother, Mr. Armstrong, say that you were very fond of parables. Now I have always had a leaning that way myself; and for years I have had one in particular glimmering before my mental sight. The ambition seized me, to write it out for one of our meetings, and so submit it to your judgment; for, Mr. Armstrong, I am so delighted with your sermons and opinions generally, that I long to let you know that I am not only friendly, but capable of sympathizing with you. But it is only in the rough yet, and I want to have plenty of time to act the dutiful bear to my offspring, and lick it into thorough shape. So if you will come this day week,

Mrs. Bloomfield and I will be delighted to entertain you in our humble fashion. But, bless me! the boys will be all in a heap of confusion worse confounded before I get back to them. I have no business to be away from them at this hour. Good morning, gentlemen."

And off ran the worthy Neptune, to quell, by the vision of his returning head, the rebellious waves of boyish impulse.

"That man will be a great comfort to you, Armstrong," I said.

"I know he will. He is a far-seeing, and what is better, a far-feeling man."

"There is true wealth in him, it seems to me, although it may be of narrow reach in expression," said I.

"I think so, quite. He seems to me to be one of those who have never grown robust because they have laboured in-doors instead of going out to work in the open air. There is a shrinking delicacy about him when with those whom he doesn't feel to be of his own kind, which makes him show to a disadvantage. But you should see him amongst his boys to do him justice."

We were interrupted by the entrance of Mrs. Armstrong, who came, after their simple fashion, to tell her husband that dinner was ready. I took my leave.

In the evening, Mrs. Bloomfield called to invite Adela and the colonel; and the affair was settled for that day week.

"You're much better, my dear, are you not?" said the worthy woman to my niece.

"Indeed I am, Mrs. Bloomfield. I could not have believed it possible that I should be so much better in so short a time--and at this season of the year too."

"Mr. Armstrong is a very clever young man, I think; though I can't say I quite relished that extraordinary story of his."

"I suppose he is clever," replied Adela, something demurely as I thought. "I must say I liked the story."

"Ah, well! Young people, you know, Mr. Smith--But, bless me! I'm sure I beg your pardon. I had forgotten you weren't a married man. Of course you're one of the young people too, Mr. Smith."

"I don't think there's much of youth to choose between you and me, Mrs. Bloomfield," said I, "if I may venture to say so. But I fear I do belong to the young people, if a liking for extravagant stories, so long as they mean well, you know--is to be the test of the classification. I fear I have a depraved taste, that way. I don't mean in this particular instance, though, Adela."

"I hope not," answered Adela, with a blushing smile, which I, at least, could read, having had not merely the key to it, but the open door and window as well, ever since I had seen the two standing together at the top of the stair.

That night the weather broke. A slow thaw set in; and before many days were over, islands of green began to appear amid the "wan water" of the snow--to use a phrase common in Scotch ballads, though with a different application. The graves in the churchyard lifted up their green altars of earth, as the first whereon to return thanks for the prophecy of spring; which, surely, if it has force and truth anywhere, speaks loudest to us in the churchyard. And on Sunday the sun broke out and shone on the green hillocks, just as good old Mr. Venables was reading the words, "I will not leave you comfortless--I will come to you."

And the ice vanished from the river, and the dark stream flowed, somewhat sullen, but yet glad at heart, on through the low meadows bordered with pollards, which, poor things, maltreated and mutilated, yet did the best they could, and went on growing wildly in all insane shapes--pitifully mingling formality and grotesqueness.

And the next day the hounds met at Castle Irksham. And that day Colonel Cathcart would ride with them.

For the good man had gathered spirit just as the light grew upon his daughter's face. And he was merry like a boy now that the first breath of spring--for so it seemed, although no doubt plenty of wintriness remained and would yet show itself--had loosened the hard hold of the frost, which is the death of Nature. The frost is hard upon old people; and the spring is so much the more genial and blessed in its sweet influences on them. Do we grow old that, in our weakness and loss of physical self-assertion, we may learn the benignities of the universe--only to be learned first through the feeling of their want?--I do not envy the man who laughs the east wind to scorn. He can never know the balmy power of its sister of the west, which is the breath of the Lord, the symbol of the one ***genial*** strength at the root of all life, resurrection, and growth--commonly called the Spirit of God.--Who has not seen, as the infirmities of age grow upon old men, the haughty, self-reliant spirit that had neglected, if not despised the gentle ministrations of love, grow as it were a little scared, and begin to look about for some kindness; begin to return the warm pressure of the hand, and to submit to be waited upon by the anxiety of love? Not in weakness alone comes the second childhood upon men, but often in childlikeness; for in old age as in nature, to quote the song of the curate,

Old Autumn's fingers Paint in hues of Spring.

The necessities of the old man prefigure and forerun the dawn of the immortal childhood. For is not our necessity towards God our highest blessedness--the fair cloud that hangs over the summit of existence? Thank God, he has made his children so noble and high that they cannot do without Him! I believe we are sent into this world just to find this out.

But to leave my reflections and return to my story--such as it is. The colonel mounted me on an old horse of his, "whom," to quote from Sir Philip Sidney's ***Arcadia***, "though he was near twenty years old, he preferred for a piece of sure service, before a great number of younger." Now the piece of sure service, in the present instance, was to take care of old John Smith, who was only a middling horseman, though his friend, the colonel, would say that he rode pretty well for a lad. The old horse, in fact, knew not only what he could do, but what I could do, for our powers were about equal. He looked well about for the gaps and the narrow places. From weakness in his forelegs, he had become a capital buck-jumper, as I think Cathcart called him, always alighting over a hedge on his hind legs, instead of his fore ones, which was as much easier for John Smith as for Hop o' my Thumb--that was the name of the old horse, he being sixteen hands, at least. But I beg my reader's pardon for troubling him with all this about my horse, for, assuredly, neither he nor I will perform any deed of prowess in his presence. But I have the weakness of garrulity in regard to a predilection from the indulgence of which circumstances have debarred me.

At nine o'clock my friend and I started upon hacks for the meet. Now, I am not going to describe the "harrow and weal away!" with which the soul of poor Reynard is hunted out of the world--if, indeed, such a clever wretch can have a soul. I daresay--I hope, at least, that the argument of the fox-hunter is analogically just, who, being expostulated with on the cruelty of fox-hunting, replied--"Well, you know, the hounds like it; and the horses like it; and there's no doubt the men like it--and who knows whether the fox doesn't like it too?" But I would not have introduced the subject except for the sake of what my reader will find in the course of a page or two, and which assuredly is not fox-hunting.

We soon found. But just before, a sudden heavy noise, coming apparently from a considerable distance, made one or two of the company say, with passing curiosity: "What is that?" It was instantly forgotten, however, as soon as the fox broke cover. He pointed towards Purley-bridge. We had followed for some distance, circumstances permitting Hop o' my Thumb to keep in the wake of his master, when the colonel, drawing rein, allowed me--I ought to say ***us***, for the old horse had quite as much voice in the matter as I had--to come up with him.

"The cunning old dog!" said he. "He has run straight for the deepest cutting in the railway. They'll all be pounded presently! They don't know this part so well as I do. I know every field and gate in it. I used to go larking over it all when I was only a cub myself. Confound it! I'm not up to much to-day. I suppose I'm getting old, you know; or I'd strike off here at right angles to the left, and make for the bridge at Crumple's Corner. I should lose the hounds though, I fear. I wonder what his lordship will do."

All the time my old friend was talking, we were following the rest of the field, whom, sure enough, as soon as we got into the next inclosure, we saw drawing up one after another on the top of the railway cutting, which ran like the river of death between them and the fox-hunter's paradise. But at the moment we entered this field, whom should we see approaching us at right angles, from the direction of Purleybridge, but Harry Armstrong, mounted on ***the*** mare! I rode towards him.

"Trapped, you see," said I. "Are you after the fox--or some nobler game?"

"I was going my rounds," answered Harry, "when I caught sight of the hounds. I have no very pressing case to day, so I turned a few yards out of the road to see a bit of the sport. Confound these railways!"

At the moment--and all this passed, as the story-teller is so often compelled to remind his reader, in far less time than it takes to tell-- over the hedge on the opposite side from where Harry had entered the field, blundered a country fellow, on a great, heavy, but spirited horse, and ploughed his way up the soft furrow to where we stood.

"Doctor!" he cried, half-breathless with haste and exertion--"Doctor!"

"Well?" answered Henry, alert.

"There's a awful accident at Grubblebon Quarry, sir. Powder blowed up. Legs and arms! Good God! sir, make haste."

"Well," said Harry, whose compressed lips alone gave sign of his being ready for action, "ride to the town, and tell my housekeeper to give you bandages and wadding and oil, and splints, and whatever she knows to be needful. Are there many hurt?"

"Half a dozen alive, sir."

"Then you'd better let the other doctors know as well. And just tell my man to saddle Jilter and take him to by brother, the curate. He had better come out at once. Ride now."

"I ***will***, sir," said the man, and was over the hedge in another minute.

But not before Harry was over the railway. For he rode gently towards it, as if nothing particular was to be done, and chose as the best spot one close to where several of the gentlemen stood, disputing for a moment as to which was the best way to get across. Now on the top of the cutting there was a rail, and between the rail and the edge of the cutting a space of about four feet. Harry trotted his mare gently up to the rail, and went over. Nor was the mutual confidence of mare and master misplaced from either side. She lighted and stood stock still within a foot of the slope, so powerful was she to stop herself. An uproar of cries arose among the men. I heard the old soldier's voice above them all.

"Damn you, Armstrong, you fool!" he cried; "you'll break your neck, and serve you right too!"

I don't know a stronger proof that the classical hell has little hold on the faith of the Saxons, than that good-hearted and true men will not unfrequently damn their friends when they are most anxious to save them. But before the words were half out of the colonel's mouth, Harry was half-way down the cutting. He had gone straight at it like a cat, and it was of course the only way. I had galloped to the edge after him, and now saw him, or rather her, descending by a succession of rebounds--not bounds--a succession, in fact, of short falls upon the fore-legs, while Harry's head was nearly touching her rump. Arrived at the bottom, she gave two bounds across the rails, and the same moment was straining right up the opposite bank in a fierce agony of effort, Harry hanging upon her neck. Now the mighty play of her magnificent hind quarters came into operation. I could see, plainly enough across the gulf, the alternate knotting and loosening of the thick muscles as, step by step, she tore her way up the grassy slope. It was a terrible trial of muscle and wind, and very few horses could have stood it. As she neared the top, her pace grew slower and slower, and the exertion more and more severe. If she had given in, she would have rolled to the bottom, but nothing was less in her thoughts. Her master never spurred or urged her, except it may have been by whispering in her ear, to which his mouth was near enough: he knew she needed no excitement to that effort. At length the final heave of her rump, as it came up to a level with her withers, told the breathless spectators that the attempt was a success, when a loud "Hurrah for the doctor and his mare!" burst from their lips. The doctor, however, only waved his hand in acknowledgment, for he had all to do yet. Fortunately there was space enough between the edge and the fence on that side to allow of his giving his mare a quarter of a circle of a gallop before bringing her up to the rail, else in her fatigue she might have failed to top it. Over she went and away, with her tail streaming out behind her, as if she had done nothing worth thinking about, once it was done. One more cheer for the doctor--but no one dared to follow him. They scattered in different directions to find a less perilous crossing. I stuck by my leader.

"By Jove! Cathcart," said Lord Irksham, as they parted, "that doctor of yours is a hero. He ought to have been bred a soldier."

"He's better employed, my lord," bawled the old colonel; for they were now a good many yards asunder, making for different points in the hedge. From this answer, I hoped well for the doctor. At all events, the colonel admired his manliness more than ever, and that was a great thing. For me, I could hardly keep down the expression of an excitement which I did not wish to show. It was a great relief to me when the ***hurrah!*** arose, and I could let myself off in that way. I told you, kind reader, I was only an old boy. But, as the Arabs always give God thanks when they see a beautiful woman, and quite right too! so, in my heart, I praised God who had made a mare with such muscles, and a man with such a heart. And I said to myself, "A fine muscle is a fine thing; but the finest muscle of all, keeping the others going too, is the heart itself. That is the true Christian muscle. And the real muscular Christianity is that which pours in a life-giving torrent from the devotion of the heart, receiving only that it may give."

But I fancy I hear my reader saying,

"Mr. Smith, you've forgotten the fox. What a sportsman you make!"

Well, I had forgotten the fox. But then we didn't kill him or find another that day. So you won't care for the rest of the run.

I was tired enough by the time we got back to Purleybridge. I went early to bed.

The next morning, the colonel, the moment we met at the breakfast table, said to me,

"You did not hear, Smith, what that young rascal of a doctor said to Lord Irksham last night?"

"No, what was it?"

"It seems they met again towards evening, and his lordship said to him: 'You hare-brained young devil!'--you know his lordship's rough way," interposed the colonel, forgetting how roundly he had sworn at Harry himself, "'by the time you're my age, you'll be more careful of the few brains you'll have left.' To which expostulated Master Harry replied: 'If your lordship had been my age, and would have done it yourself to kill a fox: when I am your lordship's age, I hope I shall have the grace left to do as much to save a man.' Whereupon his lordship rejoined, holding out his hand, 'By Jove! sir, you are an honour to your profession. Come and dine with me on Monday.' And what do you think the idiot did?--Backed out of it, and wouldn't go, because he thought his lordship condescending, and he didn't want his patronage. But his lordship's not a bit like that, you know."

"Then if he isn't, he'll like Harry all the better for declining, and will probably send him a proper invitation."

And sure enough, I was right; and Harry did dine at Castle Irksham on Monday.

Adela's eyes showed clearly enough that her ears were devouring every word we had said; and the glow on her face could not be mistaken by me at least, though to another it might well appear only the sign of such an enthusiasm as one would like every girl to feel in the presence of noble conduct of any kind. She had heard the whole story last night you may be sure; and I do not doubt that the unrestrained admiration shown by her father for the doctor's conduct, was a light in her heart which sleep itself could not extinguish, and which went shining on in her dreams. Admiration of the beloved is dear to a woman. You see I like to show that although

I ***am*** an old bachelor, I know something about ***them***.

I met Harry that morning; that is, I contrived to meet him.

"Well, how are you to-day, Harry?" I said.

"All right, thank you."

"Were there many hurt at the quarry?"

"Oh! it wasn't so very bad, I'm happy to say."

"You did splendidly yesterday."

"Oh, nonsense! It was my mare. It wasn't me. I had nothing to do with it."

"Well! well! you have my full permission to say so, and to think so, too."

"Well! well! say no more about it."

So it was long before the subject was again alluded to by me. But it will be long, too, before it is forgotten in that county.

And so the evening came when we were to meet--for the last time as the Story-telling club--at the schoolmaster's house. It was now past the time I had set myself for returning to London, and although my plans were never of a very unalterable complexion, seeing I had the faculty of being able to write wherever I was, and never admitted chairs and tables, and certain rows of bookshelves, to form part of my mental organism, without which the rest of the mechanism would be thrown out of gear, I had yet reasons for wishing to be in London; and I intended to take my departure on the day but one after the final meeting.--I may just remark, that before this time one or two families had returned to Purleybridge, and others were free from their Christmas engagements, who would have been much pleased to join our club; but, considering its ephemeral nature, and seeing it had been formed only for what we hoped was a passing necessity, we felt that the introduction of new blood, although essential for the long life of anything constituted for long life, would only hasten the decay of its butterfly constitution. So we had kept our meetings entirely to ourselves.

We all arrived about the same time, and found our host and hostess full of quiet cordiality, to which their homeliness lent an additional charm. The relation of host and guest is weakened by every addition to a company, and in a large assembly all but disappears. Indeed, the tendency of the present age is to blot from the story of every-day life all reminders of the ordinary human relations, as commonplace and insignificant, and to mingle all society in one concourse of atoms, in which the only distinctions shall be those of ***rank***; whereas the sole power to keep social intercourse from growing stale is the recognition of the immortal and true in all the simple human relations. Then we look upon all men with reverence, and find ourselves safe and at home in the midst of divine intents, which may be violated and striven with, but can never be escaped, because the will of God is the very life and well-being of his creatures.

Mrs. Bloomfield looked very nice in her black silk dress, and collar and cuffs of old lace, as she presided at the tea-table, and made us all feel that it was a pleasure to her to serve us.

After repeated apologies, and confessions of failure, our host then read the following ***parable***, as he called it, though I daresay it would be more correct to call it an ***allegory***. But as that word has so many wearisome associations, I, too, intend, whether right or wrong, to call it a parable. So, then, it shall be:

"THE CASTLE: A PARABLE.

"On the top of a high cliff, forming part of the base of a great mountain, stood a lofty castle. When or how it was built, no man knew; nor could any one pretend to understand its architecture. Every one who looked upon it felt that it was lordly and noble; and where one part seemed not to agree with another, the wise and modest dared not to call them incongruous, but presumed that the whole might be constructed on some higher principle of architecture than they yet understood. What helped them to this conclusion was, that no one had ever seen the whole of the edifice; that, even of the portion best known, some part or other was always wrapped in thick folds of mist from the mountain; and that, when the sun shone upon this mist, the parts of the building that appeared through the vaporous veil were strangely glorified in their indistinctness, so that they seemed to belong to some aerial abode in the land of the sunset; and the beholders could hardly tell whether they had ever seen them before, or whether they were now for the first time partially revealed.

"Nor, although it was inhabited, could certain information be procured as to its internal construction. Those who dwelt in it often discovered rooms they had never entered before--yea, once or twice,--whole suites of apartments, of which only dim legends had been handed down from former times. Some of them expected to find, one day, secret places, filled with treasures of wondrous jewels; amongst which they hoped to light upon Solomon's ring, which had for ages disappeared from the earth, but which had controlled the spirits, and the possession of which made a man simply what a man should be, the king of the world. Now and then, a narrow, winding stair, hitherto untrodden, would bring them forth on a new turret, whence new prospects of the circumjacent country were spread out before them. How many more of these there might be, or how much loftier, no one could tell. Nor could the foundations of the castle in the rock on which it was built be determined with the smallest approach to precision. Those of the family who had given themselves to exploring in that direction, found such a labyrinth of vaults and passages, and endless successions of down-going stairs, out of one underground space into a yet lower, that they came to the conclusion that at least the whole mountain was perforated and honeycombed in this fashion. They had a dim consciousness, too, of the presence, in those awful regions, of beings whom they could not comprehend. Once they came upon the brink of a great black gulf, in which the eye could see nothing but darkness: they recoiled with horror; for the conviction flashed upon them that that gulf went down into the very central spaces of the earth, of which they had hitherto been wandering only in the upper crust; nay, that the seething blackness before them had relations mysterious, and beyond human comprehension, with the far-off voids of space, into which the stars dare not enter.

"At the foot of the cliff whereon the castle stood, lay a deep lake, inaccessible save by a few avenues, being surrounded on all sides with precipices which made the water look very black, although it was pure as the night-sky. From a door in the castle, which was not to be otherwise entered, a broad flight of steps, cut in the rock, went down to the lake, and disappeared below its surface. Some thought the steps went to the very bottom of the water.

"Now in this castle there dwelt a large family of brothers and sisters. They had never seen their father or mother. The younger had been educated by the elder, and these by an unseen care and ministration, about the sources of which they had, somehow or other, troubled themselves very little--for what people are accustomed to, they regard as coming from nobody; as if help and progress and joy and love were the natural crops of Chaos or old Night. But Tradition said that one day--it was utterly uncertain ***when***--their father would come, and leave them no more; for he was still alive, though where he lived nobody knew. In the meantime all the rest had to obey their eldest brother, and listen to his counsels.

"But almost all the family was very fond of liberty, as they called it; and liked to run up and down, hither and thither, roving about, with neither law nor order, just as they pleased. So they could not endure their brother's tyranny, as they called it. At one time they said that he was only one of themselves, and therefore they would not obey him; at another, that he was not like them, and could not understand them, and ***therefore*** they would not obey him. Yet, sometimes, when he came and looked them full in the face, they were terrified, and dared not disobey, for he was stately and stern and strong. Not one of them loved him heartily, except the eldest sister, who was very beautiful and silent, and whose eyes shone as if light lay somewhere deep behind them. Even she, although she loved him, thought him very hard sometimes; for when he had once said a thing plainly, he could not be persuaded to think it over again. So even she forgot him sometimes, and went her own ways, and enjoyed herself without him. Most of them regarded him as a sort of watchman, whose business it was to keep them in order; and so they were indignant and disliked him. Yet they all had a secret feeling that they ought to be subject to him; and after any particular act of disregard, none of them could think, with any peace, of the old story about the return of their father to his house. But indeed they never thought much about it, or about their father at all; for how could those who cared so little for their brother, whom they saw every day, care for their father whom they had never seen?--One chief cause of complaint against him was that he interfered with their favourite studies and pursuits; whereas he only sought to make them give up trifling with earnest things, and seek for truth, and not for amusement, from the many wonders around them. He did not want them to turn to other studies, or to eschew pleasures; but, in those studies, to seek the highest things most, and other things in proportion to their true worth and nobleness. This could not fail to be distasteful to those who did not care for what was higher than they. And so matters went on for a time. They thought they could do better without their brother; and their brother knew they could not do at all without him, and tried to fulfil the charge committed into his hands.

"At length, one day, for the thought seemed to strike them simultaneously, they conferred together about giving a great entertainment in their grandest rooms to any of their neighbours who chose to come, or indeed to any inhabitants of the earth or air who would visit them. They were too proud to reflect that some company might defile even the dwellers in what was undoubtedly the finest palace on the face of the earth. But what made the thing worse, was, that the old tradition said that these rooms were to be kept entirely for the use of the owner of the castle. And, indeed, whenever they entered them, such was the effect of their loftiness and grandeur upon their minds, that they always thought of the old story, and could not help believing it. Nor would the brother permit them to forget it now; but, appearing suddenly amongst them, when they had no expectation of being interrupted by him, he rebuked them, both for the indiscriminate nature of their invitation, and for the intention of introducing any one, not to speak of some who would doubtless make their appearance on the evening in question, into the rooms kept sacred for the use of the unknown father. But by this time their talk with each other had so excited their expectations of enjoyment, which had previously been strong enough, that anger sprung up within them at the thought of being deprived of their hopes, and they looked each other in the eyes; and the look said: 'We are many and he is one--let us get rid of him, for he is always finding fault, and thwarting us in the most innocent pleasures;--as if we would wish to do anything wrong!' So without a word spoken, they rushed upon him; and although he was stronger than any of them, and struggled hard at first, yet they overcame him at last. Indeed some of them thought he yielded to their violence long before they had the mastery of him; and this very submission terrified the more tender-hearted amongst them. However, they bound him; carried him down many stairs, and, having remembered an iron staple in the wall of a certain vault, with a thick rusty chain attached to it, they bore him thither, and made the chain fast around him. There they left him, shutting the great gnarring brazen door of the vault, as they departed for the upper regions of the castle.

"Now all was in a tumult of preparation. Every one was talking of the coming festivity; but no one spoke of the deed they had done. A sudden paleness overspread the face, now of one, and now of another; but it passed away, and no one took any notice of it; they only plied the task of the moment the more energetically. Messengers were sent far and near, not to individuals or families, but publishing in all places of concourse a general invitation to any who chose to come on a certain day, and partake for certain succeeding days of the hospitality of the dwellers in the castle. Many were the preparations immediately begun for complying with the invitation. But the noblest of their neighbours refused to appear; not from pride, but because of the unsuitableness and carelessness of such a mode. With some of them it was an old condition in the tenure of their estates, that they should go to no one's dwelling except visited in person, and expressly solicited. Others, knowing what sort of persons would be there, and that, from a certain physical antipathy, they could scarcely breathe in their company, made up their minds at once not to go. Yet multitudes, many of them beautiful and innocent as well as gay, resolved to appear.

"Meanwhile the great rooms of the castle were got in readiness--that is, they proceeded to deface them with decorations; for there was a solemnity and stateliness about them in their ordinary condition, which was at once felt to be unsuitable for the light-hearted company so soon to move about in them with the self-same carelessness with which men walk abroad within the great heavens and hills and clouds. One day, while the workmen were busy, the eldest sister, of whom I have already spoken, happened to enter, she knew not why. Suddenly the great idea of the mighty halls dawned upon her, and filled her soul. The so-called decorations vanished from her view, and she felt as if she stood in her father's presence. She was at one elevated and humbled. As suddenly the idea faded and fled, and she beheld but the gaudy festoons and draperies and paintings which disfigured the grandeur. She wept and sped away. Now it was too late to interfere, and things must take their course. She would have been but a Cassandra- prophetess to those who saw but the pleasure before them. She had not been present when her brother was imprisoned; and indeed for some days had been so wrapt in her own business, that she had taken but little heed of anything that was going on. But they all expected her to show herself when the company was gathered; and they had applied to her for advice at various times during their operations.

"At length the expected hour arrived, and the company began to assemble. It was a warm summer evening. The dark lake reflected the rose-coloured clouds in the west, and through the flush rowed many gaily painted boats, with various coloured flags, towards the massy rock on which the castle stood. The trees and flowers seemed already asleep, and breathing forth their sweet dream-breath. Laughter and low voices rose from the breast of the lake to the ears of the youths and maidens looking forth expectant from the lofty windows. They went down to the broad platform at the top of the stairs in front of the door to receive their visitors. By degrees the festivities of the evening commenced. The same smiles flew forth both at eyes and lips, darting like beams through the gathering crowd. Music, from unseen sources, now rolled in billows, now crept in ripples through the sea of air that filled the lofty rooms. And in the dancing halls, when hand took hand, and form and motion were moulded and swayed by the indwelling music, it governed not these alone, but, as the ruling spirit of the place, every new burst of music for a new dance swept before it a new and accordant odour, and dyed the flames that glowed in the lofty lamps with a new and accordant stain. The floors bent beneath the feet of the time-keeping dancers. But twice in the evening some of the inmates started, and the pallor occasionally common to the household overspread their faces, for they felt underneath them a counter-motion to the dance, as if the floor rose slightly to answer their feet. And all the time their brother lay below in the dungeon, like John the Baptist in the castle of Herod, when the lords and captains sat around, and the daughter of Herodias danced before them. Outside, all around the castle, brooded the dark night unheeded; for the clouds had come up from all sides, and were crowding together overhead. In the unfrequent pauses of the music, they might have heard, now and then, the gusty rush of a lonely wind, coming and going no one could know whence or whither, born and dying unexpected and unregarded.

"But when the festivities were at their height, when the external and passing confidence which is produced between superficial natures by a common pleasure was at the full, a sudden crash of thunder quelled the music, as the thunder quells the noise of the uplifted sea. The windows were driven in, and torrents of rain, carried in the folds of a rushing wind, poured into the halls. The lights were swept away; and the great rooms, now dark within, were darkened yet more by the dazzling shoots of flame from the vault of blackness overhead. Those that ventured to look out of the windows saw, in the blue brilliancy of the quick-following jets of lightning, the lake at the foot of the rock, ordinarily so still and so dark, lighted up, not on the surface only, but down to half its depth; so that, as it tossed in the wind, like a tortured sea of writhing flames, or incandescent half-molten serpents of brass, they could not tell whether a strong phosphorescence did not issue from the transparent body of the waters, as if earth and sky lightened together, one consenting source of flaming utterance.

"Sad was the condition of the late plastic mass of living form that had flowed into shape at the will and law of the music. Broken into individuals, the common transfusing spirit withdrawn, they stood drenched, cold, and benumbed, with clinging garments; light, order, harmony, purpose departed, and chaos restored; the issuings of life turned back on their sources, chilly and dead. And in every heart reigned the falsest of despairing convictions, that this was the only reality, and that was but a dream. The eldest sister stood with clasped hands and down-bent head, shivering and speechless, as if waiting for something to follow. Nor did she wait long. A terrible flash and thunder-peal made the castle rock; and in the pausing silence that followed, her quick sense heard the rattling of a chain far off, deep down; and soon the sound of heavy footsteps, accompanied with the clanking of iron, reached her ear. She felt that her brother was at hand. Even in the darkness, and amidst the bellowing of another deep-bosomed cloud-monster, she knew that he had entered the room. A moment after, a continuous pulsation of angry blue light began, which, lasting for some moments, revealed him standing amidst them, gaunt, haggard, and motionless; his hair and beard untrimmed, his face ghastly, his eyes large and hollow. The light seemed to gather around him as a centre. Indeed some believed that it throbbed and radiated from his person, and not from the stormy heavens above them. The lightning had rent the wall of his prison, and released the iron staple of his chain, which he had wound about him like a girdle. In his hand he carried an iron fetter-bar, which he had found on the floor of the vault. More terrified at his aspect than at all the violence of the storm, the visitors, with many a shriek and cry, rushed out into the tempestuous night. By degrees, the storm died away. Its last flash revealed the forms of the brothers and sisters lying prostrate, with their faces on the floor, and that fearful shape standing motionless amidst them still.

"Morning dawned, and there they lay, and there he stood. But at a word from him, they arose and went about their various duties, though listlessly enough. The eldest sister was the last to rise; and when she did, it was only by a terrible effort that she was able to reach her room, where she fell again on the floor. There she remained lying for days. The brother caused the doors of the great suite of rooms to be closed, leaving them just as they were, with all the childish adornment scattered about, and the rain still falling in through the shattered windows. 'Thus let them lie,' said he, 'till the rain and frost have cleansed them of paint and drapery: no storm can hurt the pillars and arches of these halls.'

"The hours of this day went heavily. The storm was gone, but the rain was left; the passion had departed, but the tears remained behind. Dull and dark the low misty clouds brooded over the castle and the lake, and shut out all the neighbourhood. Even if they had climbed to the loftiest known turret, they would have found it swathed in a garment of clinging vapour, affording no refreshment to the eye, and no hope to the heart. There was one lofty tower that rose sheer a hundred feet above the rest, and from which the fog could have been seen lying in a grey mass beneath; but that tower they had not yet discovered, nor another close beside it, the top of which was never seen, nor could be, for the highest clouds of heaven clustered continually around it. The rain fell continuously, though not heavily, without; and within, too, there were clouds from which dropped the tears which are the rain of the spirit. All the good of life seemed for the time departed, and their souls lived but as leafless trees that had forgotten the joy of the summer, and whom no wind prophetic of spring had yet visited. They moved about mechanically, and had not strength enough left to wish to die.

"The next day the clouds were higher, and a little wind blew through such loopholes in the turrets as the false improvements of the inmates had not yet filled with glass, shutting out, as the storm, so the serene visitings of the heavens. Throughout the day, the brother took various opportunities of addressing a gentle command, now to one and now to another of his family. It was obeyed in silence. The wind blew fresher through the loopholes and the shattered windows of the great rooms, and found its way, by unknown passages, to faces and eyes hot with weeping. It cooled and blessed them.--When the sun arose the next day, it was in a clear sky.

"By degrees, everything fell into the regularity of subordination. With the subordination came increase of freedom. The steps of the more youthful of the family were heard on the stairs and in the corridors more light and quick than ever before. Their brother had lost the terrors of aspect produced by his confinement, and his commands were issued more gently, and oftener with a smile, than in all their previous history. By degrees his presence was universally felt through the house. It was no surprise to any one at his studies, to see him by his side when he lifted up his eyes, though he had not before known that he was in the room. And although some dread still remained, it was rapidly vanishing before the advances of a firm friendship. Without immediately ordering their labours, he always influenced them, and often altered their direction and objects. The change soon evident in the household was remarkable. A simpler, nobler expression was visible on all the countenances. The voices of the men were deeper, and yet seemed by their very depth more feminine than before; while the voices of the women were softer and sweeter, and at the same time more full and decided. Now the eyes had often an expression as if their sight was absorbed in the gaze of the inward eyes; and when the eyes of two met, there passed between those eyes the utterance of a conviction that both meant the same thing. But the change was, of course, to be seen more clearly, though not more evidently, in individuals.

"One of the brothers, for instance, was very fond of astronomy. He had his observatory on a lofty tower, which stood pretty clear of the others, towards the north and east. But hitherto, his astronomy, as he had called it, had been more of the character of astrology. Often, too, he might have been seen directing a heaven-searching telescope to catch the rapid transit of a fiery shooting-star, belonging altogether to the earthly atmosphere, and not to the serene heavens. He had to learn that the signs of the air are not the signs of the skies. Nay, once, his brother surprised him in the act of examining through his longest tube a patch of burning heath upon a distant hill. But now he was diligent from morning till night in the study of the laws of the truth that has to do with stars; and when the curtain of the sunlight was about to rise from before the heavenly worlds which it had hidden all day long, he might be seen preparing his instruments with that solemn countenance with which it becometh one to look into the mysterious harmonies of Nature. Now he learned what law and order and truth are, what consent and harmony mean; how the individual may find his own end in a higher end, where law and freedom mean the same thing, and the purest certainty exists without the slightest constraint. Thus he stood on the earth, and looked to the heavens.

"Another, who had been much given to searching out the hollow places and recesses in the foundations of the castle, and who was often to be found with compass and ruler working away at a chart of the same which he had been in process of constructing, now came to the conclusion, that only by ascending the upper regions of his abode could he become capable of understanding what lay beneath;

and that, in all probability, one clear prospect, from the top of the highest attainable turret, over the castle as it lay below, would reveal more of the idea of its internal construction, than a year spent in wandering through its subterranean vaults. But the fact was, that the desire to ascend wakening within him had made him forget what was beneath; and having laid aside his chart for a time at least, he was now to be met in every quarter of the upper parts, searching and striving upward, now in one direction, now in another; and seeking, as he went, the best outlooks into the clear air of outer realities.

"And they began to discover that they were all meditating different aspects of the same thing; and they brought together their various discoveries, and recognized the likeness between them; and the one thing often explained the other, and combining with it helped to a third. They grew in consequence more and more friendly and loving; so that every now and then one turned to another and said, as in surprise, 'Why, you are my brother!'--'Why, you are my sister!' And yet they had always known it.

"The change reached to all. One, who lived on the air of sweet sounds, and who was almost always to be found seated by her harp or some other instrument, had, till the late storm, been generally merry and playful, though sometimes sad. But for a long time after that, she was often found weeping, and playing little simple airs which she had heard in childhood-- backward longings, followed by fresh tears. Before long, however, a new element manifested itself in her music. It became yet more wild, and sometimes retained all its sadness, but it was mingled with anticipation and hope. The past and the future merged in one; and while memory yet brought the rain-cloud, expectation threw the rainbow across its bosom-- and all was uttered in her music, which rose and swelled, now to defiance, now to victory; then died in a torrent of weeping.

"As to the eldest sister, it was many days before she recovered from the shock. At length, one day, her brother came to her, took her by the hand, led her to an open window, and told her to seat herself by it, and look out. She did so; but at first saw nothing more than an unsympathizing blaze of sunlight. But as she looked, the horizon widened out, and the dome of the sky ascended, till the grandeur seized upon her soul, and she fell on her knees and wept. Now the heavens seemed to bend lovingly over her, and to stretch out wide cloud-arms to embrace her; the earth lay like the bosom of an infinite love beneath her, and the wind kissed her cheek with an odour of roses. She sprang to her feet, and turned, in an agony of hope, expecting to behold the face of the father, but there stood only her brother, looking calmly though lovingly on her emotion. She turned again to the window. On the hilltops rested the sky: Heaven and Earth were one; and the prophecy awoke in her soul, that from betwixt them would the steps of the father approach.

"Hitherto she had seen but Beauty; now she beheld Truth. Often had she looked on such clouds as these, and loved the strange ethereal curves into which the winds moulded them; and had smiled as her little pet sister told her what curious animals she saw in them, and tried to point them out to her. Now they were as troops of angels, jubilant over her new birth, for they sang, in her soul, of beauty, and truth, and love. She looked down, and her little sister knelt beside her.

"She was a curious child, with black, glittering eyes, and dark hair; at the mercy of every wandering wind; a frolicsome, daring girl, who laughed more than she smiled. She was generally in attendance on her sister, and was always finding and bringing her strange things. She never pulled a primrose, but she knew the haunts of all the orchis tribe, and brought from them bees and butterflies innumerable, as offerings to her sister. Curious moths and glow-worms were her greatest delight; and she loved the stars, because they were like the glow-worms. But the change had affected her too; for her sister saw that her eyes had lost their glittering look, and had become more liquid and transparent. And from that time she often observed that her gaiety was more gentle, her smile more frequent, her laugh less bell-like; and although she was as wild as ever, there was more elegance in her motions, and more music in her voice. And she clung to her sister with far greater fondness than before.

"The land reposed in the embrace of the warm summer days. The clouds of heaven nestled around the towers of the castle; and the hearts of its inmates became conscious of a warm atmosphere--of a presence of love. They began to feel like the children of a household, when the mother is at home. Their faces and forms grew daily more and more beautiful, till they wondered as they gazed on each other. As they walked in the gardens of the castle, or in the country around, they were often visited, especially the eldest sister, by sounds that no one heard but themselves, issuing from woods and waters; and by forms of love that lightened out of flowers, and grass, and great rocks. Now and then the young children would come in with a slow, stately step, and, with great eyes that looked as if they would devour all the creation, say that they had met the father amongst the trees, and that he had kissed them; 'And,' added one of them once, 'I grew so big!' But when the others went out to look, they could see no one. And some said it must have been the brother, who grew more and more beautiful, and loving, and reverend, and who had lost all traces of hardness, so that they wondered they could ever have thought him stern and harsh. But the eldest sister held her peace, and looked up, and her eyes filled with tears. 'Who can tell,' thought she, 'but the little children know more about it than we?'

"Often, at sunrise, might be heard their hymn of praise to their unseen father, whom they felt to be near, though they saw him not. Some words thereof once reached my ear through the folds of the music in which they floated, as in an upward snowstorm of sweet sounds. And these are some of the words I heard--but there was much I seemed to hear which I could not understand, and some things which I understood but cannot utter again.

"'We thank thee that we have a father, and not a maker; that thou hast begotten us, and not moulded us as images of clay; that we have come forth of thy heart, and have not been fashioned by thy hands. It ***must*** be so. Only the heart of a father is able to create. We rejoice in it, and bless thee that we know it. We thank thee for thyself. Be what thou art--our root and life, our beginning and end, our all in all. Come home to us. Thou livest; therefore we live. In thy light we see. Thou art--that is all our song.'

"Thus they worship, and love, and wait. Their hope and expectation grow ever stronger and brighter, that one day, ere long, the Father will show Himself amongst them, and thenceforth dwell in His own house for evermore. What was once but an old legend has become the one desire of their hearts.

"And the loftiest hope is the surest of being fulfilled."

* * * * *

"Thank you, heartily," said the curate. "I will choose another time to tell you how much I have enjoyed your parable, which is altogether to my mind, and far beyond anything I could do."

Mr. Bloomfield returned no answer, but his countenance showed that he was far from hearing this praise unmoved. The faces of the rest showed that they too had listened with pleasure; and Adela's face shone as if she had received more than delight--hope, namely, and onward impulse. The colonel alone--I forgot to say that Mrs. Cathcart had a headache, and did not come--seemed to have been left behind.

"I am a stupid old fellow, I believe," said he; "but to tell the truth, I did not know what to make of it. It seemed all the time to be telling me in one breath something I knew and something I didn't and couldn't know. I wish I could express what I mean, but it puzzled me too much for that; although every now and then it sounded very beautiful indeed."

"I will try and tell you what it said to me, sometime, papa," said Adela.

"Thank you, my child; I should much like to understand it. I believe I have done my duty by my king and country, but a man has to learn a good deal after all that is over and done with; and I suppose it is never too late to begin, Mr. Armstrong?"

"On the contrary, I not merely believe that no future time can be so good as the present, but I am inclined to assert that no past time could have been so good as the present. This seems to be a paradox, but I think I could explain it very easily. I find, however, that the ladies are looking as if they wanted to go home, and I am quite ready, Mrs. Armstrong. But while the ladies put their bonnets on, just let Smith see your schoolroom, Mr. Bloomfield. As an inhabitant of Purleybridge, I already begin to be proud of it."

The ladies did go to put on their bonnets. I followed Mr. Bloomfield and the colonel into the schoolroom, and the curate followed me. But after we had looked about us and remarked on the things about for five minutes, finding I had left my handkerchief in the drawing-room, I went back to fetch it. The door was open, and I saw Adela--no bonnet on her head yet-- standing face to face with Harry. They were alone. I hesitated for a moment what I should do, and while I hesitated, I could not help seeing the arm of the doctor curved and half-outstretched, as if it would gladly have folded about her, and his face droop and droop, till it could not have been more than half a foot from hers. Now, as far as my seeing this was concerned, there was no harm done. But behind me came the curate and the schoolmaster, and they had eyes in their heads, at least equal to mine. Well, no great harm yet. And just far enough down the stair to see into the drawing-room, appeared their wives, who could not fail to see the unconscious pair, at least as well as we men below. Still there was no great harm done, for Mrs. Cathcart was at home, as I have said. But, ***horresco referens!*** excuse the recondite quotation--at the same moment the form of the colonel appeared, looking over the heads of all before him right in at the drawing-room door, and full at the young sinners, who had heard no sound along the matted passage.

"Here's a go!" said I to myself--not aloud, observe, for it was slang.

For just think of a man like Harry caught thus in a perfect trap of converging looks.

As if from a sudden feeling of hostile presence, he glanced round--and stood erect. The poor fellow's face at once flushed as red as shame could make it, but he neither lost his self-possession, nor sought to escape under cover of a useless pretence. He turned to the colonel.

"Colonel Cathcart," he said, "I will choose a more suitable time to make my apology. I wish you good night."

He bowed to us all, not choosing to risk a refusal of his hand by the colonel, and went quickly out of the house.

The colonel stood for some moments, which felt to me like minutes, as if he had just mounted guard at the drawing-room door. His face was perfectly expressionless. We men felt very much like stale oysters, and would rather have skipped that same portion of our inevitable existence. What the ladies felt, I do not pretend, being an old bachelor, to divine.

Adela, pale as death, fled up the stair. The only thing left for the rest of us was, to act as much as possible as if nothing were the matter, and get out of the way before the poor girl came down again. As soon as I got home, I went to my own room, and thus avoided the ***tete-a-tete*** with my host which generally closed our evenings.

The colonel went up to his daughter's room, and remained there for nearly an hour. Adela was not at the breakfast-table the next morning. Her father looked very gloomy, and Mrs. Cathcart grimly satisfied, with ***I told you so*** written on her face as plainly as I have now written it on the paper. How she came to know anything about it, I can only conjecture.

CHAPTER VIII. WHAT NEXT?

Harry called early, and was informed that the colonel was not at home. "Something's the matter, Mr. Armstrong," said Beeves. "Master's not at home to you to-day, he says, nor any other day till he countermands the order--that was the word, sir. I'm sure I am very sorry, sir."

"So am I," said Harry. "How's your mistress?"

"Haven't seen her to-day, sir. Emma says she's poorly. But she is down. Emma looks as if she knew something and wouldn't tell it. I'll get it out of her though, sir. We'll be having that old Wade coming about the house again, I'm afeard, sir. ***He's*** no good."

"At all events you will let your master know that I have called," said Harry, as he turned disconsolately, to take his departure.

"That I will, sir. And I'll be sure he hears me. He's rather deaf, sometimes, you know, sir."

"Thank you, Beeves. Good morning."

Now what could have been Harry's intention in calling upon the colonel? Why, as he had said himself, to make an apology. But what kind of apology could he make? Clearly there was only one that would satisfy all parties-- and that must be in the form of a request to be allowed to pay his addresses--(that used to be the phrase in my time--I don't know the young ladies' slang for it now-a-days)--to Adela. Did I say--satisfy all parties? This was just the one form affairs might take, which would least of all satisfy the colonel. I believe, with all his rigid proprieties, he would have preferred the confession that the doctor had so far forgotten himself as to attempt to snatch a kiss--a theft of which I cannot imagine a gentleman guilty, least of all a doctor from his patient; which relation no doubt the colonel persisted in regarding as the sole possible and everlastingly permanent one between Adela and Harry. The former was, however, the only apology Harry could make; and evidently the colonel expected it when he refused to see him.

But why should he refuse to see him?--The doctor was not on an equality with the colonel. Well, to borrow a form from the Shorter Catechism: wherein consisted the difference between the colonel and the doctor?--The difference between the colonel and the doctor consisted chiefly in this, that whereas the colonel lived by the wits of his ancestors, Harry lived by his own, and therefore was not so respectable as the colonel. Or in other words: the colonel inherited a good estate, with the ordinary quantity of brains; while Harry inherited a good education and an extraordinary quantity of brains. So of course it was very presumptuous in Harry to aspire to the hand of Miss Cathcart.

In the forenoon the curate called upon me, and was shown into the library where I was.

"What's that scapegrace brother of mine been doing, Smith?" he asked, the moment he entered.

"Wanting to marry Adela," I replied.

"What has he done?"

"Called this morning."

"And seen Colonel Cathcart?"

"No."

"Not at home?"

"In a social sense, not at home; in a moral sense, very far from at home; in a natural sense, seated in his own arm-chair, with his own work on the Peninsular War open on the table before him."

"Wouldn't see him?"

"No."

"What's he to do then?"

"I think we had better leave that to him. Harry is not the man I take him for if he doesn't know his own way better than you or I can tell him."

"You're right, Smith. How's Miss Cathcart?"

"I have never seen her so well. Certainly she did not come down to breakfast, but I believe that was merely from shyness. She appeared in the dining-room directly after, and although it was evident she had been crying, her step was as light and her colour as fresh as her lover even could wish to see them."

"Then she is not without hope in the matter?"

"If she loves him, and I think she does, she is not without hope. But I do not think the fact of her looking well would be sufficient to prove that. For some mental troubles will favour the return of bodily health. They will at least give one an interest in life."

"Then you think her father has given in a little about it?"

"I don't believe it.--If her illness and she were both of an ordinary kind, she would gain her point now by taking to her bed. But from what I know of Adela she would scorn and resist that."

"Well, we must let matters take their course. Harry is worthy of the best wife in Christendom."

"I believe it. And more, if Adela will make that best wife, I think he will have the best wife. But we must have patience."

Next morning, a letter arrived from Harry to the colonel. I have seen it, and it was to this effect:

"My dear Sir,--As you will not see me, I am forced to write to you. Let my earnest entreaty to be allowed to address your daughter, cover, if it cannot make up for, my inadvertence of the other evening. I am very sorry I have offended you. If you will receive me, I trust you will not find it hard to forget. Yours, &c."

To this the colonel replied:

"Sir,--It is at least useless, if not worse, to apply for an ***ex post facto*** permission. What I might have answered, had the courtesies of society been observed, it may be easy for me to determine, but it is useless now to repeat. Allow me to say that I consider such behaviour of a medical practitioner towards a young lady, his patient, altogether unworthy of a gentleman, as every member of a learned profession is supposed to be. I have the honour, &c."

I returned the curate's call, and while we were sitting in his study, in walked Harry with a rather rueful countenance.

"What do you say to that, Ralph?" said he, handing his brother the letter.

"Cool," replied Ralph. "But Harry, my boy, you have given him quite the upper hand of you. How could you be so foolish as kiss the girl there and then?"

"I didn't," said Harry.

"But you did just as bad. You were going to do it."

"I don't think I was. But somehow those great eyes of hers kept pulling and pulling my head, so that I don't know what I was going to do. I remember nothing but her eyes. Suddenly a scared look in them startled me, and I saw it all. Mr. Smith, was it so very dishonourable of me?"

"You are the best judge of that yourself, Harry," I answered. "Just let me look at the note."

I read it, folded it up carefully, and returning it, said:

"He's given you a good hold of him there. It is really too bad of Cathcart, being a downright good fellow, to forget that he ran away with Miss Selby, old Sir George, the baronet's daughter. Neither of them ever repented it; though he was only Captain Cathcart then, in a regiment of foot, too, and was not even next heir to the property he has now."

"Hurrah!" cried Harry.

"Stop, stop. That doesn't make it a bit better," said his brother. "I suppose you mean to argue with him on that ground, do you?"

"No, I don't. I'm not such a fool. But if I ***should*** be forced to run away with her, ***he*** can't complain, you know."

"No, no, Harry, my boy," said I. "That won't do. It would break the old man's heart. You must have patience for a while."

"Yes, yes. I know what I mean to do."

"What?"

"When I've made up my mind, I never ask advice. It only bewilders a fellow."

"Quite right, Hal," said his brother. "Only don't do anything foolish."

"I won't do anything she doesn't like."

"No, nor anything you won't like yourself afterwards," I ventured to say.

"I hope not," returned he, gravely, as he walked out, too much absorbed to bid either of us ***good morning***.

It was now more than time that I should return to town; but I could not leave affairs in this unsatisfactory state. I therefore lingered on to see what would come next.

CHAPTER IX.
GENERALSHIP.

The next day Harry called again.

"Master 'aint countermanded the order, Doctor. He 'aint at home--not a bit of it. He 'aint been out of the house since that night."

"Well, is Miss Cathcart at home?"

"She's said nothing to the contrairy, sir. I believe she ***is*** at home. I know she's out in the garding--on the terridge."

And old Beeves held the door wide open, as if to say--"Don't stop to ask any questions, but step into the garden." Which Harry did.

There was a high gravel terrace along one end of it, always dry and sunny when there was any sun going; and there she was, over-looked by the windows of her papa's room.

Now I do not know anything that passed upon that terrace. How should I know? Neither of them was likely to tell old Smith. And I wonder at the clumsiness of novelists in pretending to reveal all that ***he*** said, and all that ***she*** answered. But if I were such a clumsy novelist, I should like to invent it all, and see if I couldn't make you believe every word of it.

This is what I would invent.

The moment Adela caught sight of Harry, she cast one frightened glance up to her father's windows, and stood waiting. He lifted his hat; and held out his hand. She took it. Neither spoke. They turned together and walked along the terrace.

"I am very sorry," said Harry at last.

"Are you? What for?"

"Because I got you into a scrape."

"Oh! I don't care."

"Don't you?"

"No; not a bit."

"I didn't mean it."

"What didn't you mean?"

"It did look like it, I know."

"Look like what?"

"Adela, you'll drive me crazy. It was all your fault."

"So I told papa, and he was angrier than ever."

"You angel! It wasn't your fault. It was your eyes. I couldn't help it. Adela, I love you dreadfully."

"I'm ***so*** glad."

She gave a sigh as of relief.

"Why?"

"Because I wished you would. But I don't deserve it. A great clever man like you love a useless girl like me! I ***am*** so glad!"

"But your papa?"

"I'm so happy, I can't think about him steadily just yet."

"Adela, I love you--so dearly! Only I am too old for you."

"Old! how old are you?"

"Nearly thirty."

"And I'm only one-and-twenty. You're worth one and a half of me--yes twenty of me."

And so their lips played with the ripples of love, while their hearts were heaving with the ground swell of its tempest.

Now what I do know about is this:

The colonel came down-stairs in his dressing-gown and slippers, and found Beeves flattening his nose against the glass of the garden-door.

"Beeves!" said the colonel.

"Sir!" said Beeves, darting around and confronting his master with a face purple and pale from the sense of utter unpreparedness.

"Beeves, where is your mistress?"

"My mistress, sir? I beg your pardon, sir, I'm sure, sir! How should I know, sir? I 'aint let her out. Shall I run up-stairs and see if she is in her room?"

"Open the door."

Beeves laid violent hold upon the handle of the door, and pulled and twisted, but always took care to pull before he twisted.

"I declare if that stupid Ann 'aint been and locked it. It aint nice in the garden to-day, sir--leastways without goloshes," added he, looking down at his master's slippers.

Now the colonel understood Beeves, and Beeves knew that he understood him. But Beeves knew likewise that the colonel would not give in to the possibility of his servant's taking such liberties with him.

"Never mind," said the colonel; "I will go the other way."

The moment he was out of sight, Beeves opened the garden-door, and began gesticulating like a madman, fully persuaded that the doctor would make his escape. But so far from being prepared to run away, Harry had come there with the express intention of forcing a conference. So that when the colonel made his appearance on the terrace, the culprits walked slowly towards him. He went to meet them with long military strides, and was the first to speak.

"Mr. Armstrong, to what am I to attribute this intrusion?"

"Chiefly to the desire of seeing you, Colonel Cathcart."

"And I find you with my daughter!--Adela, go in-doors,"

Adela withdrew at once.

"You denied yourself, and I inquired for Miss Cathcart."

"You will oblige me by not calling again."

"Surely I have committed no fault beyond forgiveness."

"You have taken advantage of your admission into my family to entrap the affections of my daughter."

"Colonel Cathcart, as far as my conscience tells me, I have not behaved unworthily."

"Sir, is it not unworthy of a gentleman to use such professional advantages to gain the favour of one who--you will excuse me for reminding you of what you will not allow me to forget--is as much above him in social position, as inferior to him in years and experience."

"Is it always unworthy in a gentleman to aspire to a lady above him in social position, Colonel Cathcart?"

The honesty of the colonel checked all reply to this home-thrust.

Harry resumed:

"At least I am able to maintain my wife in what may be considered comfort."

"Your wife!" exclaimed the colonel, his anger blazing out at the word. "If you use that expression with any prospective reference to Miss Cathcart, I am master enough in my own family to insure you full possession of the presumption. I wish you good morning."

The angry man of war turned on his slippered heel, and was striding away.

"One word, I beg," said Harry.

The colonel had too much courtesy in his nature not to stop and turn half towards the speaker.

"I beg to assure you," said Harry, "that I shall continue to cherish the hope that after-thoughts will present my conduct, as well as myself, in a more favourable light to Colonel Cathcart."

And he lifted his hat, and walked away by the gate.

"By Jove!" said the colonel, to himself, notwithstanding the rage he was in, "the fellow can express himself like a gentleman, anyhow."

And so he went back to his room, where I heard him pacing about for hours. I believe he found that his better self was not to be so easily put down as he had supposed; and that that better self sided with Adela and Harry.

CHAPTER X.
AN UNFORESEEN FORESIGHT.

What else is a Providence?

Harry went about his work as usual, only with a graver face.

Adela looked very sad, but without any of her old helpless and hopeless air. Her health was quite established; and she now returned all the attention her father had paid to her.--Fortunately Mrs. Cathcart had gone home.

"Cunning puss!" some of my readers may say; "she was trying to coax the old man out of his resolution." But such a notion would be quite unjust to my niece. She was more in danger of going to the other extreme, to avoid hypocrisy. But she had the divine gift of knowing what any one she loved was feeling and thinking; and she knew that her father was suffering, and all about it. The old man's pace grew heavier; the lines about his mouth grew deeper; he sat at table without speaking; he ate very little, and drank more wine. Adela's eyes followed his every action. I could see that sometimes she was ready to rise and throw her arms about him. Often I saw in her lovely eyes that peculiar clearness of the atmosphere which indicates the nearness of rain. And once or twice she rose and left the room, as if to save her from an otherwise unavoidable exposure of her feelings.

The gloom fell upon the servants too. Beeves waited in a leaden-handed way, that showed he was determined to do his duty, although it should bring small pleasure with it. He took every opportunity of unburdening his bosom to me.

"It's just like when mis'ess died," said he. "The very cocks walk about the yard as if they had hearse-plumes in their tails. Everybody looks ready to hang hisself, except you, Mr. Smith. And that's a comfort."

The fact was, that I had very little doubt as to how it would all end. But I would not interfere; for I saw that it would be much better for the colonel's heart and conscience to right themselves, than that he should be persuaded to anything, it was very hard for him. He had led his regiment to victory and glory; he had charged and captured many a gun; he had driven the enemy out of many a boldly defended entrenchment; and was it not hard that he could not drive the ***eidolon*** of a country surgeon out of the bosom of his little girl? (It was hard that he could not; but it would have been a deal harder if he could). He had nursed and loved, and petted and spoiled her. And she ***would*** care for a man whom he disliked!

But here the old man was mistaken. He did not dislike Harry Armstrong. He admired and honoured him. He almost loved him for his gallant devotion to his duty. He would have been proud of him for a son--but not for a son-in-law. He would not have minded adopting him, or doing anything ***but*** giving him Adela. There was a great deal of pride left in the old soldier, and that must be taken out of him. We shall all have to thank God for the whip of scorpions which, if needful, will do its part to drive us into the kingdom of heaven.

"How happy the dear old man will be," I said to myself, "when he just yields this last castle of selfishness, and walks unhoused into the new childhood, of which God takes care!"

And this end came sooner than I had looked for it.

I had made up my mind that it would be better for me to go.

When I told Adela that I must go, she gave me a look in which lay the whole story in light and in tears. I answered with a pressure of her hand and an old uncle's kiss. But no word was spoken on the subject.

I had a final cigar with the curate, and another with the schoolmaster; bade them and their wives good-bye; told them all would come right if we only had patience, and then went to Harry. But he was in the country, and I thought I should not see him again.

With the assistance of good Beeves, I got my portmanteau packed that night. I was going to start about ten o'clock next morning. It was long before I got to sleep, and I heard the step of the colonel, whose room was below mine on the drawing-room floor, going up and down, up and down, all the time, till slumber came at last, and muffled me up.--We met at breakfast, a party lugubrious enough. Beeves waited like a mute; the colonel ate his breakfast like an offended parent; Adela trifled with hers like one who had other things to think about; and I ate mine like a parting guest who was being anything but sped. When the postbag was brought in, the colonel unlocked it mechanically; distributed the letters; opened one with indifference, read a few lines, and with a groan fell back in his chair. We started up, and laid him on the sofa. With the privilege of an old friend, I glanced at the letter, and found that a certain speculation in which the colonel had ventured largely, had utterly failed. I told Adela enough to satisfy her as to the nature of the misfortune. We feared apoplexy, but before we could send for any medical man, he opened his eyes, and called Adela. He clasped her to his bosom, and then tried to rise; but fell back helpless.

"Shall we send for Dr. Wade?" said Adela, trembling and pale as death.

"Dr. Wade!" faltered the old man, with a perceptible accent of scorn.

"Which shall we send for?" I said.

"How can you ask?" he answered, feebly. "Harry Armstrong, of course."

The blood rushed into Adela's white face, and Beeves rushed out of the room. In a quarter of an hour, Harry was with us. Adela had retired. He made a few inquiries, administered some medicine he had brought with him, and, giving orders that he should not be disturbed for a couple of hours, left him with the injunction to keep perfectly quiet.

"Take my traps up to my room again, Beeves: and tell the coach-man he won't be wanted this morning."

"Thank you, sir," said Beeves. "I don't know what we should do without you, sir."

When Harry returned, we carried the colonel up to his own room, and Beeves got him to bed. I said something about a nurse, but Harry said there was no one so fit to nurse him as Adela. The poor man had never been ill before; and I daresay he would have been very rebellious, had he not had a great trouble at his heart to quiet him. He was as submissive as could be desired.

I felt sure he would be better as soon as he had told Adela. I gave Harry a hint of the matter, and he looked very much as if he would shout "Oh, jolly!" but he did not.

Towards the evening, the colonel called his daughter to his bedside, and said,

"Addie, darling, I have hurt you dreadfully."

"Oh, no! dear papa; you have not. And it is so easy to put it all right, you know," she added, turning her head away a little.

"No, my child," he said in a tone full of self-reproach, "nobody can put it right. I have made us both beggars, Addie, my love."

"Well, dearest papa, you can bear a little poverty surely?"

"It's not of myself I am thinking, my darling. Don't do me that injustice, or I shall behave like a fool. It's only you I am thinking of."

"Oh, is that all, papa? Do you know that, if it were not for your sake, I could sing a song about it!"

"Ah! you don't know what you make so light of. Poverty is not so easy to endure."

"Papa," said Adela, solemnly, "if you knew how awful things looked to me a little while ago--but it's all gone now!--the whole earth black and frozen to the heart, with no God in it, and nothing worth living for--you would not wonder that I take the prospect of poverty with absolute indifference--yes, if you will believe me, with something of a strange excitement. There will be something to battle with and beat."

And she stretched out a strong, beautiful white arm--from which the loose open sleeve fell back, as if with that weapon of might she would strike poverty to the earth; but it was only to adjust the pillow, which had slipped sideways from the loved head.

"But Mr. Armstrong will not want to marry you now, Addie."

"Oh, won't he?" thought Adela; or at least I think she thought so. But she said, rather demurely, and very shyly:

"But that won't be any worse than it was before; for you know you would never have let me marry him anyhow."

"Oh! yes, I would, in time, Adela. I am not such a brute as you take me for."

"Oh! you dear darling papa!" cried the poor child, and burst into tears, with her head on her father's bosom. And he began comforting her so sweetly, that you would have thought she had lost everything, and he was going to give her all back again.

"Papa! papa!" she cried, "I will work for you; I will be your servant; I will love you and love you to all eternity. I won't leave you. I won't indeed. What ***does*** it matter for the money!"

At this moment the doctor entered.

"Ah!" he said, "this won't do at all. I thought you would have made a better nurse, Miss Adela. There you are, both crying together!"

"Indeed, Mr. Henry," said Adela, rather comically, "it's not my fault. He would cry."

And as she spoke she wiped away her own tears.

"But he's looking much better, after all," said Harry. "Allow me to feel your pulse."

The patient was pronounced much better; fresh orders were given; and Harry took his leave.

But Adela felt vexed. She did not consider that he knew nothing of what had passed between her father and her. To the warm fire-side of her knowledge, he came in wintry and cold. Of course it would never do for the doctor to aggravate his patient's symptoms by making love to his daughter; but ought he not to have seen that it was all right between them now?--How often we feel and act as if our mood were the atmosphere of the world! It may be a cold frost within us, when our friend is in the glow of a summer sunset: and we call him unsympathetic and unfeeling. If we let him know the state of our world, we should see the rosehues fade from his, and our friend put off his singing robes, and sit down with us in sackcloth and ashes, to share our temptation and grief.

"You see I cannot offer you to him now, Adela," said her father.

"No, papa."

But I knew that all had come right, although I saw from Adela's manner that she was not happy about it.

So things went on for a week, during which the colonel was slowly mending. I used to read him to sleep. Adela would sit by the fire, or by the bedside, and go and come while I was reading.

One afternoon, in the twilight, Harry entered. We greeted; and then, turning to the bed, I discovered that my friend was asleep. We drew towards the fire, and sat down. Adela had gone out of the room a few minutes before.

"He is such a manageable patient!" I said.

"Noble old fellow!" returned the doctor. "I wish he would like me, and then all would be well."

"He doesn't dislike you personally," I said.

"I hope not. I can understand his displeasure perfectly, and repugnance too. But I assure you, Mr. Smith, I did not lay myself out to gain her affections. I was caught myself before I knew. And I believe she liked me too before she knew."

"I fear their means will be very limited after this."

"For his sake I am very sorry to hear it; but for my own, I cannot help thinking it the luckiest thing that could have happened."

"I am not so sure of that. It might increase the difficulty."

At this moment I thought I heard the handle of the door move, but there was a screen between us and it. I went on.

"That is, if you still want to marry her, you know."

"Marry her!" he said. "If she were a beggar-maid, I would be proud as King Cophetua to marry her to-morrow."

There was a rustle in the twilight, and a motion of its gloom. With a quick gliding, Adela drew near, knelt beside Harry, and hid her eyes on his knee. I thought it better to go.

Was this unmaidenly of her?

I say "No, for she knew that he loved her."

As I left the room, I heard the colonel call--

"Adela."

And when I returned, I found them both standing by the bedside, and the old man holding a hand of each.

"Now, John Smith," I said to myself, "you may go when you please."

Before we, that is, I and my reader, part, however, my reader may be inclined to address me thus:

"Pray, Mr. Smith, do you think it was your wonderful prescription of story-telling, that wrought Miss Cathcart's cure?"

"How can I tell?" I answer. "Probably it had its share. But there were other things to take into the account. If you went on to ask me whether it was not Harry's prescriptions; or whether it was not the curate's sermons; or whether it was not her falling in love with the doctor; or whether even her father's illness and the loss of their property had not something to do with it; or whether it was not the doctor's falling in love with her; or that the cold weather suited her; I should reply in the same way to every one of the interrogatories."

But I retort another question:

"Did you ever know anything whatever resulting from the operation of one separable cause?"

In regard to any good attempt I have ever made in my life, I am content to know that the end has been gained. Whether ***I*** have succeeded or not is of no consequence, if I have tried well.--In the present case, Adela recovered; and my own conviction is, that the cure was effected mainly from within. Except in physics, we can put nothing to the ***experimentum crucis***, and must be content with conjecture and probability.

The night before I left, I had a strange dream. I stood in a lonely cemetery in a pine-forest. Dark trees that never shed their foliage rose all around--strange trees that mourn for ever, because they never die. The dream light that has no visible source, because it is in the soul that dreams, showed all in a dim blue-grey dawn, that never grew clearer. The night wind was the only power abroad save myself. It went with slow intermitting, sigh-like gusts, through the tops of the dreaming trees; for the trees seemed, in the midst of my dream, to have dreams of their own.

Now this burial-place was mine. I had tended it for years. In it lay all the men and women whom I had honoured and loved.

And I was a great sculptor. And over every grave I had placed a marble altar, and upon every altar the marble bust of the man or woman who lay beneath; each in the supreme beauty which all the defects of birth and of time and of incompleteness, could not hide from the eye of the prophetic sculptor. Each was like a half-risen glorified form of the being who had there descended into the realms of Hades. And through these glimmering rows of the dead I walked in the dream-light; and from one to another I went in the glory of having known and loved them; now weeping sad tears over the loss of the beautiful; now rejoicing in the strength of the mighty; now exulting in the love and truth which would yet dawn upon me when I too should go down beneath the visible, and emerge in the realms of the actual and the unseen? All the time I was sensible of a wondrous elevation of being, a glory of life and feeling hitherto unknown to me.

I had entered the secret places of my own hidden world by the gate of sleep, and walked about them in my dream.

Gradually I became aware that a foreign sound was mingling with the sighing of the tree-tops overhead. It grew and grew, till I recognized the sound of wheels--not of heavenly chariots, but of earthly motion and business. I heard them stop at the lofty gates of my holy place, and by twoes and threes, or in solitary singleness, came people into my garden of the dead. And who should they be but the buried ones?--all those whose marble busts stood in ghostly silence, within the shadows of the everlasting pines? And they talked and laughed and jested. And my city of the dead melted away. And lo! we stood in the midst of a great market-place; and I knew it to be the market-place in which the children had sat who said to the other children:

"We have piped unto you, and ye have not danced; we have mourned unto you, and ye have not lamented."

And to my misery, I saw that the faces of my fathers and brothers, my mothers and sisters, had not grown nobler in the country of the dead, in which I had thought them safe and shining. Cares, as of this world, had so settled upon them, that I could hardly recognize the old likeness; and the dim forms of the ideal glory which I had reproduced in my marble busts, had vanished altogether. Ah me! my world of the dead! my city of treasures, hid away under the locks and bars of the unchangeable! Was there then no world of realities?--only a Vanity Fair after all? The glorious women went sweeping about, smiling and talking, and buying and adorning, but they were glorious no longer; for they had common thoughts, and common beauties, and common language and aims and hopes; and everything was common about them. And ever and anon, with a kind of shiver, as if to keep alive my misery by the sight of my own dreams, the marble busts would glimmer out, faintly visible amidst the fair, as if about to reappear, and, dispossessing the vacuity of folly, assert the noble and the true, and give me back my dead to love and worship once more, in the loneliness of the pine-forest. Side by side with a greedy human face, would shimmer out for a moment the ghostly marble face; and the contrast all but drove me mad with perplexity and misery.

"Alas!" I cried, "where is my future? Where is my beautiful death?"

All at once I saw the face of a man who went round and round the skirts of the market, and looked earnestly in amongst the busy idlers. He was head and shoulders taller than any there; and his face was a pale face, with an infinite future in it, visible in all its grief. I made my way through the crowd, which regarded me with a look which I could not understand, and came to the stranger. I threw myself at his feet and sobbed: "I have lost them all. I will follow thee." He took me by the hand, and led me back. We walked up and down the fair together. And as we walked, the tumult lessened, and lessened. They made a path for us to go, and all eyes were turned upon my guide. The tumult sank, and all was still. Men and women stood in silent rows. My guide looked upon them all, on the right and on the left. And they all looked on him till their eyes filled with tears. And the old faces of my friends grew slowly out of the worldly faces, until at length they were such as I had known of yore.

Suddenly they all fell upon their knees, and their faces changed into the likeness of my marble faces. Then my guide waved his hand--and lo! we were in the midst of my garden of the dead; and the wind was like the sound of a going in the tops of the pine trees; and my white marbles glimmered glorified on the altars of the tombs. And the dream vanished, and I came awake.

And I will not say here whose face the face of my guide was like.

The Codes Of Hammurabi And Moses
W. W. Davies

QTY

The discovery of the Hammurabi Code is one of the greatest achievements of archaeology, and is of paramount interest, not only to the student of the Bible, but also to all those interested in ancient history...

Religion **ISBN:** ***1-59462-338-4*** **Pages:132**
MSRP ***$12.95***

The Theory of Moral Sentiments
Adam Smith

QTY

This work from 1749. contains original theories of conscience amd moral judgment and it is the foundation for systemof morals.

Philosophy **ISBN:** ***1-59462-777-0*** **Pages:536**
MSRP ***$19.95***

Jessica's First Prayer
Hesba Stretton

QTY

In a screened and secluded corner of one of the many railway-bridges which span the streets of London there could be seen a few years ago, from five o'clock every morning until half past eight, a tidily set-out coffee-stall, consisting of a trestle and board, upon which stood two large tin cans, with a small fire of charcoal burning under each so as to keep the coffee boiling during the early hours of the morning when the work-people were thronging into the city on their way to their daily toil...

Pages:84
Childrens **ISBN:** ***1-59462-373-2*** *MSRP* ***$9.95***

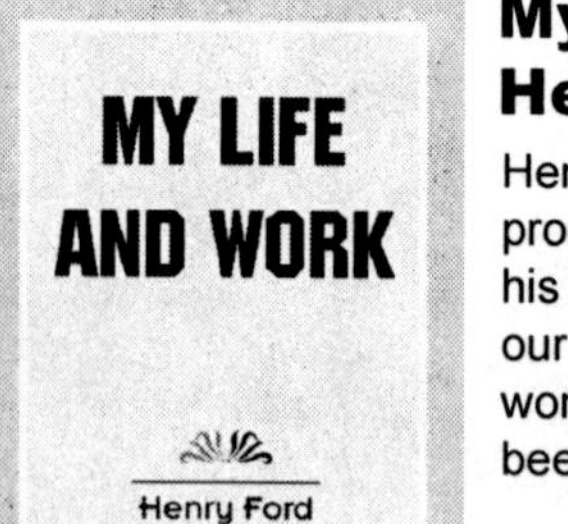

My Life and Work
Henry Ford

QTY

Henry Ford revolutionized the world with his implementation of mass production for the Model T automobile. Gain valuable business insight into his life and work with his own auto-biography... "We have only started on our development of our country we have not as yet, with all our talk of wonderful progress, done more than scratch the surface. The progress has been wonderful enough but..."

Pages:300
Biographies/ **ISBN:** ***1-59462-198-5*** *MSRP* ***$21.95***

The Art of Cross-Examination
Francis Wellman

QTY

I presume it is the experience of every author, after his first book is published upon an important subject, to be almost overwhelmed with a wealth of ideas and illustrations which could readily have been included in his book, and which to his own mind, at least, seem to make a second edition inevitable. Such certainly was the case with me; and when the first edition had reached its sixth impression in five months, I rejoiced to learn that it seemed to my publishers that the book had met with a sufficiently favorable reception to justify a second and considerably enlarged edition. ..

Pages:412

Reference **ISBN: *1-59462-647-2*** *MSRP* ***$19.95***

On the Duty of Civil Disobedience
Henry David Thoreau

QTY

Thoreau wrote his famous essay, On the Duty of Civil Disobedience, as a protest against an unjust but popular war and the immoral but popular institution of slave-owning. He did more than write—he declined to pay his taxes, and was hauled off to gaol in consequence. Who can say how much this refusal of his hastened the end of the war and of slavery ?

Law **ISBN: *1-59462-747-9*** **Pages:48**

MSRP ***$7.45***

Dream Psychology Psychoanalysis for Beginners
Sigmund Freud

QTY

Dream Psychology
Psychoanalysis for Beginners
Sigmund Freud

Sigmund Freud, born Sigismund Schlomo Freud (May 6, 1856 - September 23, 1939), was a Jewish-Austrian neurologist and psychiatrist who co-founded the psychoanalytic school of psychology. Freud is best known for his theories of the unconscious mind, especially involving the mechanism of repression; his redefinition of sexual desire as mobile and directed towards a wide variety of objects; and his therapeutic techniques, especially his understanding of transference in the therapeutic relationship and the presumed value of dreams as sources of insight into unconscious desires.

Pages:196

Psychology **ISBN: *1-59462-905-6*** *MSRP* ***$15.45***

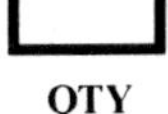

The Miracle of Right Thought
Orison Swett Marden

QTY

Believe with all of your heart that you will do what you were made to do. When the mind has once formed the habit of holding cheerful, happy, prosperous pictures, it will not be easy to form the opposite habit. It does not matter how improbable or how far away this realization may see, or how dark the prospects may be, if we visualize them as best we can, as vividly as possible, hold tenaciously to them and vigorously struggle to attain them, they will gradually become actualized, realized in the life. But a desire, a longing without endeavor, a yearning abandoned or held indifferently will vanish without realization.

Pages:360

Self Help **ISBN: *1-59462-644-8*** *MSRP* ***$25.45***

www.bookjungle.com *email: sales@bookjungle.com fax: 630-214-0564 mail: Book Jungle PO Box 2226 Champaign, IL 61825*

QTY

The Rosicrucian Cosmo-Conception Mystic Christianity *by* ***Max Heindel*** **ISBN:** ***1-59462-188-8*** **$38.95**
The Rosicrucian Cosmo-conception is not dogmatic, neither does it appeal to any other authority than the reason of the student. It is: not controversial, but is: sent forth in the, hope that it may help to clear... *New Age/Religion Pages 646*

Abandonment To Divine Providence *by* ***Jean-Pierre de Caussade*** **ISBN:** ***1-59462-228-0*** **$25.95**
"The Rev. Jean Pierre de Caussade was one of the most remarkable spiritual writers of the Society of Jesus in France in the 18th Century. His death took place at Toulouse in 1751. His works have gone through many editions and have been republished... *Inspirational/Religion Pages 400*

Mental Chemistry ***by Charles Haanel*** **ISBN:** ***1-59462-192-6*** **$23.95**
Mental Chemistry allows the change of material conditions by combining and appropriately utilizing the power of the mind. Much like applied chemistry creates something new and unique out of careful combinations of chemicals the mastery of mental chemistry... *New Age Pages 354*

The Letters of Robert Browning and Elizabeth Barret Barrett 1845-1846 vol II **ISBN:** ***1-59462-193-4*** **$35.95**
by ***Robert Browning*** *and* ***Elizabeth Barrett***
Biographies Pages 596

Gleanings In Genesis (volume I) *by* ***Arthur W. Pink*** **ISBN:** ***1-59462-130-6*** **$27.45**
Appropriately has Genesis been termed "the seed plot of the Bible" for in it we have, in germ form, almost all of the great doctrines which are afterwards fully developed in the books of Scripture which follow... *Religion/Inspirational Pages 420*

The Master Key *by* ***L. W. de Laurence*** **ISBN:** ***1-59462-001-6*** **$30.95**
In no branch of human knowledge has there been a more lively increase of the spirit of research during the past few years than in the study of Psychology, Concentration and Mental Discipline. The requests for authentic lessons in Thought Control, Mental Discipline and... *New Age/Business Pages 422*

The Lesser Key Of Solomon Goetia *by* ***L. W. de Laurence*** **ISBN:** ***1-59462-092-X*** **$9.95**
This translation of the first book of the "Lernegton" which is now for the first time made accessible to students of Talismanic Magic was done, after careful collation and edition, from numerous Ancient Manuscripts in Hebrew, Latin, and French... *New Age/Occult Pages 92*

Rubaiyat Of Omar Khayyam *by* ***Edward Fitzgerald*** **ISBN:***1-59462-332-5* **$13.95**
Edward Fitzgerald, whom the world has already learned, in spite of his own efforts to remain within the shadow of anonymity, to look upon as one of the rarest poets of the century, was born at Bredfield, in Suffolk, on the 31st of March, 1809. He was the third son of John Purcell... *Music Pages 172*

Ancient Law *by* ***Henry Maine*** **ISBN:** ***1-59462-128-4*** **$29.95**
The chief object of the following pages is to indicate some of the earliest ideas of mankind, as they are reflected in Ancient Law, and to point out the relation of those ideas to modern thought. *Religiom/History Pages 452*

Far-Away Stories *by* ***William J. Locke*** **ISBN:** ***1-59462-129-2*** **$19.45**
"Good wine needs no bush, but a collection of mixed vintages does. And this book is just such a collection. Some of the stories I do not want to remain buried for ever in the museum files of dead magazine-numbers an author's not unpardonable vanity..." *Fiction Pages 272*

Life of David Crockett ***by David Crockett*** **ISBN:** ***1-59462-250-7*** **$27.45**
"Colonel David Crockett was one of the most remarkable men of the times in which he lived. Born in humble life, but gifted with a strong will, an indomitable courage, and unremitting perseverance... *Biographies/New Age Pages 424*

Lip-Reading *by* ***Edward Nitchie*** **ISBN:** ***1-59462-206-X*** **$25.95**
Edward B. Nitchie, founder of the New York School for the Hard of Hearing, now the Nitchie School of Lip-Reading, Inc, wrote "LIP-READING Principles and Practice". The development and perfecting of this meritorious work on lip-reading was an undertaking... *How-to Pages 400*

A Handbook of Suggestive Therapeutics, Applied Hypnotism, Psychic Science **ISBN:** ***1-59462-214-0*** **$24.95**
by Henry Munro
Health/New Age/Health/Self-help Pages 376

A Doll's House: and Two Other Plays *by* ***Henrik Ibsen*** **ISBN:** ***1-59462-112-8*** **$19.95**
Henrik Ibsen created this classic when in revolutionary 1848 Rome. Introducing some striking concepts in playwriting for the realist genre, this play has been studied the world over. *Fiction/Classics/Plays 308*

The Light of Asia *by* ***sir Edwin Arnold*** **ISBN:** ***1-59462-204-3*** **$13.95**
In this poetic masterpiece, Edwin Arnold describes the life and teachings of Buddha. The man who was to become known as Buddha to the world was born as Prince Gautama of India but he rejected the worldly riches and abandoned the reigns of power when... *Religion/History/Biographies Pages 170*

The Complete Works of Guy de Maupassant *by* ***Guy de Maupassant*** **ISBN:** ***1-59462-157-8*** **$16.95**
"For days and days, nights and nights, I had dreamed of that first kiss which was to consecrate our engagement, and I knew not on what spot I should put my lips..." *Fiction/Classics Pages 240*

The Art of Cross-Examination *by* ***Francis L. Wellman*** **ISBN:** ***1-59462-309-0*** **$26.95**
Written by a renowned trial lawyer, Wellman imparts his experience and uses case studies to explain how to use psychology to extract desired information through questioning. *How-to/Science/Reference Pages 408*

Answered or Unanswered? *by* ***Louisa Vaughan*** **ISBN:** ***1-59462-248-5*** **$10.95**
Miracles of Faith in China
Religion Pages 112

The Edinburgh Lectures on Mental Science (1909) *by* ***Thomas*** **ISBN:** ***1-59462-008-3*** **$11.95**
This book contains the substance of a course of lectures recently given by the writer in the Queen Street Hail, Edinburgh. Its purpose is to indicate the Natural Principles governing the relation between Mental Action and Material Conditions... *New Age/Psychology Pages 148*

Ayesha *by* ***H. Rider Haggard*** **ISBN:** ***1-59462-301-5*** **$24.95**
Verily and indeed it is the unexpected that happens! Probably if there was one person upon the earth from whom the Editor of this, and of a certain previous history, did not expect to hear again... *Classics Pages 380*

Ayala's Angel *by* ***Anthony Trollope*** **ISBN:** ***1-59462-352-X*** **$29.95**
The two girls were both pretty, but Lucy who was twenty-one who supposed to be simple and comparatively unattractive, whereas Ayala was credited, as her Bombwhat romantic name might show, with poetic charm and a taste for romance. Ayala when her father died was nineteen... *Fiction Pages 484*

The American Commonwealth *by* ***James Bryce*** **ISBN:** ***1-59462-286-8*** **$34.45**
An interpretation of American democratic political theory. It examines political mechanics and society from the perspective of Scotsman James Bryce
Politics Pages 572

Stories of the Pilgrims *by* ***Margaret P. Pumphrey*** **ISBN:** ***1-59462-116-0*** **$17.95**
This book explores pilgrims religious oppression in England as well as their escape to Holland and eventual crossing to America on the Mayflower, and their early days in New England... *History Pages 268*

CPSIA information can be obtained at www.ICGtesting.com
Printed in the USA
BVOW051054180412

287968BV00004B/87/P